He'd touched her soul...

"Why did you come get me?" she asked. "After I dropped you off at the hotel, you could have taken off when you realized everything was about to hit the fan. Why did you..." Her voice trailed off as another thought occurred to her. She was his only link to the investigation. Had he ditched her, he would have been in the clear while she led the parade in another direction. In a way he'd risked his life for her. She swallowed hard.

"Taryn?" He touched her cheek again.

She felt her protective wall begin to crumble. How long had it been since someone had taken care of her?

He started to speak again but she put a finger to his mouth to silence him. She grabbed the front of his shirt and pulled him toward her before he could guess her intention.

Their lips met with an urgency that consumed them....

Dear Harlequin Intrigue Reader,

It's autumn, and there's no better time to *fall* in love with Harlequin Intrigue!

Book two of TEXAS CONFIDENTIAL, *The Agent's Secret Child* (#585) by B.J. Daniels, will thrill you with heart-stopping suspense and passion. When secret agent Jake Cantrell is sent to retrieve a Colombian gangster's widow and her little girl, he is shocked to find the woman he'd once loved and lost—and a child who called him *Daddy*....

Nick Travis had hired missing persons expert Taryn Scott to find a client, in Debbi Rawlins's SECRET IDENTITY story, *Her Mysterious Stranger* (#587). Working so closely with the secretive Nick was dangerous to Taryn's life, for her heart was his for the taking. But when his secrets put her life at risk, Nick had no choice but to put himself in the line of fire to protect her.

Susan Kearney begins her new Western trilogy, THE SUTTON BABIES, with *Cradle Will Rock* (#586). When a family of Colorado ranchers is besieged by a secret enemy, will they be able to preserve the one thing that matters most—a future for their children?

New author Julie Miller knows all a woman needs is *One Good Man* (#588). Casey Maynard had suffered a vicious attack that scarred not only her body, but her soul. Shut up in a dreary mansion, she and sexy Mitch Taylor, the cop assigned to protect her, strike sparks off each other. Could Mitch save her when a stalker returned to finish the job? This book is truly a spine-tingling pager-turner!

As always, Harlequin Intrigue is committed to giving readers the best in romantic suspense. Next month, watch for releases from your favorite special promotions—TEXAS CONFIDENTIAL, THE SUTTON BABIES, MORE MEN OF MYSTERY and SECRET IDENTITY!

Sincerely,

Denise O'Sullivan
Associate Senior Editor
Harlequin Intrigue

HER MYSTERIOUS STRANGER

DEBBI RAWLINS

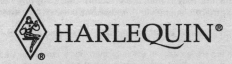

HARLEQUIN®

TORONTO • NEW YORK • LONDON
AMSTERDAM • PARIS • SYDNEY • HAMBURG
STOCKHOLM • ATHENS • TOKYO • MILAN • MADRID
PRAGUE • WARSAW • BUDAPEST • AUCKLAND

ISBN 0-373-22587-3

HER MYSTERIOUS STRANGER

Copyright © 2000 by Debbi Quattrone

This edition published by arrangement with Harlequin Books S.A.

® and TM are trademarks of the publisher. Trademarks indicated with ® are registered in the United States Patent and Trademark Office, the Canadian Trade Marks Office and in other countries.

Visit us at www.eHarlequin.com

Printed in U.S.A.

ABOUT THE AUTHOR

Debbi Rawlins currently lives with her husband and dog in Las Vegas, Nevada. A native of Hawaii, she married on Maui and has since lived in Cincinnati, Chicago, Tulsa, Houston, Detroit and Durham, NC, during the past twenty years. Now that she's had enough of the gypsy life, it'll take a crane, a bulldozer and a fork lift to get her out of her new home. Good thing she doesn't like to gamble. Except maybe on romance.

Books by Debbi Rawlins

Don't miss any of our special offers. Write to us at the following address for information on our newest releases.

Harlequin Reader Service
U.S.: 3010 Walden Ave., P.O. Box 1325, Buffalo, NY 14269
Canadian: P.O. Box 609, Fort Erie, Ont. L2A 5X3

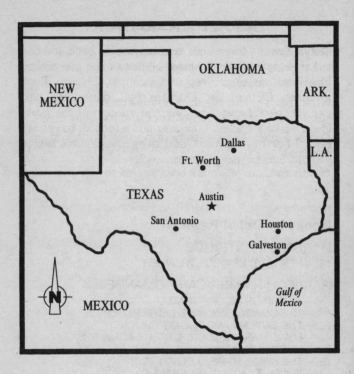

CAST OF CHARACTERS

Taryn Scott—She needs one last job to get out of the missing persons business—but will the payoff be worth the consequences?

Nick Travis—The tall, dark and handsome lawyer is suspiciously good at surveillance and handling a gun.

Dylan Sands—The missing man's trail is more than a year old.

Harrison Cain—Sands's boss seems to want to help Taryn.

Richard Cross—Harrison's assistant makes no secret of his hatred for Dylan Sands.

Archibald Hanes—Sands's neighbor seems very sure Sands will return.

Dennis Maynard—He's an unlikable boor, but does that make him a killer?

Myron "Moose" McGraw—The bartender is the only person Taryn trusts implicitly.

Syd Sebastian—He doesn't seem surprised to learn Sands might be alive.

Lucy—Taryn's daughter is her most precious secret—and her biggest weakness.

Chapter One

A full moon always meant trouble. And a slew of business for Scott Investigations. But business wasn't what occupied Taryn Scott's mind. A night like this would forever remind her of Derek's death.

She shivered in the dank barroom and stared out the window into the growing darkness. The scavengers had already descended on the vacant lot across the street, vying for places to sleep among the smashed beer cans and fast-food wrappers. The scene was familiar, no different than most evenings that she sat here at her usual spot, but sometimes it was just too painful for Taryn to watch and she dragged her restless gaze away.

Inside Myron's Place, the mood wasn't any more uplifting. A haze of smoke clouded the air, hanging heavily near the dented jukebox and pool table, where four bikers chugged tequila. In the far corner, a young man slumped in a chair, blood caking one corner of his mouth. Taryn had just walked in when the fight over a game of nine ball had ended in an explosion of temper. The guy was definitely more drunk than hurt. Otherwise she would've had to intervene. Which she hated to do. As motley a crew as this bunch was, she could usually count on them to keep the more undesirables off her back. Getting into the middle of their business wouldn't endear her to them.

"What the hell are you doing here tonight, Taryn?" Moose, alias Myron, asked in his raspy two-pack-a-day voice. Frowning at her from the opposite side of the bar, he pulled the stained white towel from over his shoulder and wiped the area in front of her. "You turned in those two bail jumpers this afternoon, didn't ya? Get out of the city for the weekend, kid."

She picked up her beer so that he could get at the sticky residue under the bottle. "What I need is to get out of this business." Shaking her head, she met his probing eyes. His steely blues softened, and the gruff bar owner almost smiled.

Her own lips curved slightly. "This time I mean it." She fisted her hand around the crushed napkin she'd been doodling on. "I figure if I collect a dozen more decent bounties, not the piddling hot-check bail jumpers' kind, I'll have enough to start over someplace. Maybe in the burbs where I can get one of those cushy nine-to-five insurance investigator jobs."

Rubbing a hand over his smooth, shiny head, Moose snorted. "You'd be bored spitless in a week."

She shrugged. "Maybe. But I can't do this anymore." She tipped the bottle up to her lips. The beer had grown too warm and it tasted bitter. Even after all these years prowling the seamier side of this godforsaken city, she still hadn't quite acquired a taste for the stuff.

"I know, kid. I know." He hesitated, his dark bushy brows drawing together as he stared at her with open concern. Not the fatherly type, Moose usually

spared her advice. Yet he was the closest person to a
father she'd had in the past twelve years, since her
parents had stopped taking her calls.

From the other end of the bar, a guy with long,
greasy hair and a gleaming gold tooth yelled for another shot of whiskey. Moose cursed under his breath
and gave Taryn an exasperated look. But since he was
the only bartender, he yelled at the guy to keep his
shirt on, then lumbered in that direction.

Taryn opened her hand and stared at the figures
she'd scratched on the napkin. Bounty hunting was
good money, but she needed a lot more than she'd
managed to stash if she wanted to get a fresh start.
Her thoughts strayed to Derek and how much of their
savings he'd blown before he'd stupidly gone and
gotten himself killed, and bitterness coated the inside
of her mouth. She smothered the resentment. It
wouldn't do her or Lucy a damn bit of good to waste
the energy.

"Aren't you going to Clear Lake this weekend?"

She looked up and saw that Moose had returned
with another beer. She didn't want it but took it, anyway. "She's on a camping trip." Taryn didn't have
to explain further. He knew she was talking about
Lucy. In fact, he was the only one she trusted to know
about her daughter. It was safer that way. "What
about you? Going anywhere?"

"Right." He swatted viciously at a fly before giving her a beefy shrug. "I got no other bartenders."

It was more than that, she knew. He probably
couldn't afford to meet payroll again. The IRS was
leaning on him for back taxes. "Hey, I could work a
shift for you. For free beer. I've got nothing better to
do."

He laughed, his round belly jiggling where his too-tight   black T-shirt didn't quite meet his jeans. "I got enough trouble keeping these lowlifes away from you, gorgeous," he said, inclining his head toward the unsavory mix of bikers and druggies who were his customers. "You don't wanna be trapped behind a bar without me here."

Her laugh was short, humorless. Tonight she felt old and worn out, not like someone who'd have to worry about being hit on. Not by a decent guy, anyway. Her innocence was long gone. She'd taken care of that the day she'd ditched finishing school to hop on the back of Derek's motorcycle. "Like I don't know how to take care of myself."

"Yeah, I know." Moose gave her a long, considering look. "You don't belong here, kid. Never have. Never will."

Avoiding his eyes, she stared at her beer. He was wrong. She belonged here, all right. Not in the suburbs, not at a PTA meeting or school bake sale... maybe once, when she'd been the good daughter, the class valedictorian, the homecoming queen, a promising Ford model, but not anymore.

She picked up the bottle but couldn't bring herself to take a sip. It was that damn full moon making her edgy, making the back of her neck prickle. Making her remember things better left tucked away in the dark corners of her mind.

"Hey, Taryn, you up for some eight ball? Twenty bucks will get you in the game."

She turned at the sound of Butch's gravelly voice. He was chalking his cue stick, a cigarette dangling from the corner of his swollen mouth. Behind him, the door opened and brightness from an outside street-light trespassed into the murky bar.

A man stepped through the doorway, his shoulders filling the space between the frame, his dark head dipping slightly to clear the top. His face was shadowed, but his tailored and expensive-looking tweed jacket wasn't. Nor was the gold watch gleaming at his wrist. He stopped briefly, the light of a bare overhead bulb shining on dark eyes that leisurely scanned the sea of worn black leather, shaggy beards and elaborate tattoos. His face remained expressionless under the weight of several hostile stares. When his eyes met Taryn's, a sudden and eerie flash of foreboding sent a vibration down her spine and she looked away.

Damn full moon.

"Are you in or not?" Butch shoved an impatient hand through his greasy black hair, his wary glance flickering toward the stranger.

More heads turned toward the man. Although he didn't look like a cop, half the guys in the bar were probably ducking outstanding warrants and got nervous when anyone new showed up. If this guy was a cop, he was a stupid one to let himself stand out. Unless he was undercover. That would account for the gold Rolex.

Involuntarily Taryn's gaze returned to him. He didn't seem the least bit intimidated by all the dark looks, or by the way Snake Eyes Jones set aside his cue stick to fold his thick arms across his burly tattooed chest and stare.

"Not tonight," she finally replied to Butch, intrigued by the confidence oozing from the stranger as he wove a slow and unhurried path through the haze of stale smoke.

When it became obvious he was headed her way, she turned back to her beer and stared straight ahead at the dusty wall mirror behind the bar. Between a bottle of Jack Daniel's and a jug of cheap wine, the man's blurred reflection allowed Taryn to track his movement. He stopped two stools down from her and signaled Moose, who'd been busy swatting at another fly.

A mixture of caution and speculation drew the bar owner's eyebrows together in a frown as he lumbered toward the stranger. "What'll it be?"

"Scotch. Neat." The man's voice was deep. Kind of husky. Self-assured. It suited him.

Moose grunted. "No Scotch."

Without responding, the stranger swung partway around and surveyed the room with a sweeping gaze that came to rest on Taryn. Grudgingly, she dragged her attention from the mirror to meet his eyes. They were brown. Not too dark. More whiskey-colored.

She gave a brief nod of acknowledgment, looked away and sipped her unwanted beer.

"I'll have one of those," he said, and out of the corner of her eye, she saw him nudge his chin in her direction. And then he laid a crisp fifty-dollar bill on the bar. "I'm looking for Derek Scott."

She nearly choked on the bitter brew, her wary gaze finding Moose's perplexed frown. Always protective of her, especially since Derek's death, he carefully avoided looking her way, uncapped a bottle of beer, slid it toward the intruder. "Yeah?" He eyed the fifty. "You got business with him?"

Clearly refusing the challenge in Moose's voice,

the man pulled out a stool, sat down and lifted his beer. "Maybe. You his secretary?"

Moose's jaw sagged in disbelief. After a brief, menacing silence, the big man gave a short bark of laughter. "Could be. What do ya want?"

"I have a job for him."

"Yeah?" Moose rested his corded forearms on the bar and leaned closer.

The other man took a long, unhurried pull of beer, and Moose quickly slid Taryn a questioning look. Before she could give him any kind of signal, the stranger set down the bottle and leaned in to meet Moose's eyes. "Tell Scott it's an easy job and my client's got deep pockets."

"Client?" Moose grunted and paused long enough to take out another fly. "I knew you weren't no cop. You a private dick?"

One side of the man's mouth lifted slowly, the action forming a crease down his clean-shaven cheek. "An attorney. With fifty bucks for anyone with the right information."

Moose scratched his protruding belly and sent the money a longing look. He started to shrug a noncommittal shoulder when a tall, braless blonde in a white tank top at the far end of the bar slammed down two empty pitchers and yelled for more beer. He shot Taryn another questioning glance as he straightened, then eyed the fifty bucks again before ambling off toward the blonde.

Immediately Taryn felt the force of the stranger's stare searing an imprint on her left cheek. She kept her face averted, carefully avoiding eye contact, and studied the figures on her crumpled napkin. She hadn't decided yet if she was interested in what the guy had to say. Since Derek's murder, she'd only hired herself out to bail bondsmen she knew and occasionally the Houston police department. Unfounded paranoia, probably, although Moose agreed with her caution. She wasn't in a position to take risks. Not now.

And this guy, no matter how well-dressed or well-spoken, was a risk. Besides being a total stranger, why had he shown up here? She had an answering service. That's how she did business. Everyone knew that. Obviously he knew enough about Scott Investigations to know that they'd always hung out here, yet he didn't know about Derek's death. And why hadn't he asked for her? She was Derek's partner...always had been. Even at the cost of her family. Her inheritance.

She relaxed the death grip on her beer and flexed her cramped fingers. She was being too touchy. If the guy was up to no good, he wouldn't show up here with two dozen witnesses—half of them willing to flatten him just for looking at her the wrong way. Not that she couldn't handle herself, she thought with amused irony. God knew she'd crawled through enough gutters to have learned how to take down a person Moose's size. Most likely this guy simply was an attorney and she'd be a fool not to hear him out...especially if his client really was loaded.

She continued to toy with the napkin while Moose filled the pitchers with beer and ogled the blonde. A small financial windfall would put Taryn ahead of the game, and she would do just about anything to put things back to right with Lucy.

Taryn slanted the stranger a sidelong glance. He was partially turned, his well-defined jaw aimed toward the back of the bar, his probing gaze canvassing the room with a confident nonchalance she found compelling. He seemed totally oblivious to the occasional but menacing stares targeting him like poison darts. Even cops normally weren't this cool. Not in a place like this. Unless…

Her gaze wandered down his body. Immediately she saw it. On the right side of his waist. The slight bulge broke the even fall of the pricey tweed fabric of his jacket. He had a gun. She'd bet her classic Harley on it.

She let out a long, slow breath. So? She had one, too. Any sane person would in this neighborhood. Of course, you had to be half nuts to hang around here in the first place.

Or desperate.

Moose appeared and started to reach for her bottle. He'd replace the lukewarm beer. She waved him away. She had a decision to make and she needed to do it with a clear head.

"Good idea. Maybe you should hit the road," he said, his gaze fastened to hers, his meaning clear.

"Maybe," she agreed, then turned to the stranger. "You'd better have a lot more than fifty bucks. Scott doesn't come cheap." She shrugged a shoulder. "Assuming you have a case worth taking."

Relaxing in his seat, the man angled toward her, his eyes brimming with amused curiosity as they rested on her face. "Money usually speaks for itself."

"Usually." She picked up her beer and briefly exchanged a glance with Moose. He didn't look happy. He thought she was being foolish. Maybe she was. But as the man said, money spoke loud and clear. "But Scott's picky."

The man pursed his lips and appeared to be giving the matter some thought, then he reached for the fifty still sitting on the bar. Taryn was quicker. She flattened her hand over the money, preventing him from taking it. The sudden move startled Moose and had him reaching under the bar for his shotgun. The stranger barely blinked. He merely shifted his hand away. Moose straightened, his weapon left beneath the bar.

Taryn waited another second to make sure everyone was cool, then she slid the money toward Moose. "He earned it," she told the attorney. "I'm your contact."

The stranger stared at her for several tense seconds, his face giving not a single emotion away. A lump started to form in her throat. She cleared it. Not many people or situations made her nervous. She didn't like that he unsettled her even the slightest. When his gaze stayed locked on her, she refused to look away. Finally, he nodded, a trace of a smile curving his mouth.

She pulled back and it took Moose barely a second to pocket the money. "This don't cover your beer," he told the man. "That's another two bucks."

The guy seemed to ignore Moose, his attention fixed unwaveringly on Taryn. He reached into his pocket, then laid a ten on the bar. "Keep it," he said, without breaking eye contact with her, then he extended his hand. "Nick Travis."

She accepted his overture, keeping the physical connection brief. "Anyone in the back room?" she asked Moose as she slid off the stool.

"Nope. It's all yours." He sent Travis a warning glance. "I'll be right here."

She gave her friend a quick smile, then led Travis

toward the small, shabby poolroom that separated the bar from the alley out back.

Two bikers near the dartboard stopped tossing back shots of tequila long enough to watch them enter the dimly lit room. All she had to do was raise her voice once and any number of the regular crowd would gladly rush in to provide this guy with a couple of new body cavities. But she doubted that would be necessary. Surely this guy was too smart to mess with her here.

She flipped the switch beside the door, then realized the light was already on. The dangling bare bulb was covered with so much dust and grime that it barely colored the faded, felt-covered pool table with a murky sheen. The air reeked of stale liquor and trapped cigarette smoke. And God knew what else.

Exhaling slowly, in a vain attempt to rid herself of the foulness, she turned to face him.

He didn't seem bothered by the putrid decor. He was too busy staring at her legs. Automatically she ran a palm down the front of her short black skirt. Not her typical work attire. Nor her usual preference. But neither was doing laundry.

"What exactly did you want, Mr. Travis?" she asked, folding her arms across her chest and staring back at him.

His gaze rose to meet her icy one. "What do I call you?"

He thought she was a go-between, and that misconception suited her fine for now. "That doesn't matter. What's the job?"

His eyes stayed focused on her a moment longer and then his attention drifted past her and fastened on something in the back of the room. He gestured with a slight jerk of his chin. "Scott?"

She didn't have to turn around to know he was referring to the door that led to the back alley. "You talk to me first," she said, purposely not correcting his faulty assumption.

When he reached into his jacket, she tensed. He paused, indicating he'd read her fear, and she silently cursed herself for the foolish display of vulnerability. "I'm getting out a business card," he said, his hand slowly starting to move again.

"The gun, too," she said, inclining her head toward his midsection. "Lay it on the table."

Surprise narrowed his eyes. "What gun?"

Arching an eyebrow at him, she decided to give him this one bluff, but if he further denied having a weapon, she'd be out of here in a heartbeat.

He didn't. A slight twitch controlled his right jaw, but he calmly reached inside his jacket, withdrew a 9 mm Glock from the waistband of his pressed designer jeans and laid it on the pool table. "For protection. I heard Houston's a rough city."

"Anything else?"

Again he stalled as if weighing a decision. No matter that it was brief, the hesitation did nothing for her peace of mind. "That's it," he said.

"Then you won't mind me patting you down." She stepped closer, making it clear she wasn't giving him a choice.

He raised his arms. "Hell, I'll probably enjoy it."

Ignoring the taunt, she started under his arms and ran both palms down his tapered torso, his trim waist. She froze when she came to a long, hard object in his jeans' pocket.

"Do you do the honors, or shall I?" he asked, with a trace of amusement that made her want to stick his gun between his ribs.

"Go. Slowly." She moved back a few inches.

Shrugging, he slid a hand into his pocket and produced a small pocketknife. Nothing that would do much damage. Still, it was a strange thing for him to be carrying.

He laid it beside the gun. "I confiscated it from my nephew earlier today," he said, his mouth curving slightly, "not that it would do much damage." His echo of her own thoughts soothed, and coaxed a tight smile of relief from her. "Unless, of course, you went for the jugular."

The sudden steeliness in his eyes sent a leap of misgiving up her spine and her smile edged away. She patted the outside of his legs. "Is that it?"

"That's it," he said, lifting his hands again, this time in mock surrender.

"Good. Now, strip."

He reacted with a bark of laughter. "You're kidding."

"Never about money or safety."

He mumbled a curse. "I came here to hire Scott. Why the shakedown?"

"You shouldn't have lied about the gun."

"I never lied. I bluffed."

"Okay," she said, nodding in concession. "Now it's going to cost you." She gave him a taunting grin. "Don't worry, Travis. Anything you've got, I've seen before."

A slow smile replaced the agitation on his face. "You sure about that?"

"Yeah." She leaned a hip against the table. The guy's self-confidence was astounding.

"Okay...whatever blows your skirt up," he said, and started to shrug out of his jacket.

She ignored the bait. No doubt he was hoping for an indignant, flustered denial resulting in him getting off the hook. The man didn't know her. She smiled to herself and continued to watch as he unfastened the top buttons of his polo shirt, then drew the fabric over his head.

The first thing she noticed was that he had a great chest. Not too muscled but well-defined. The next thing that attracted her attention was the pair of scars to the left of his navel. They were relatively small, round...something a .22 caliber would leave behind. A couple of inches higher was a longer, more faded scar. Probably from a knife. No attorney she knew led this rough a life. If that's all he really was, she'd eat that gun.

She lifted her gaze and was immediately drawn into the intensity of his scrutiny. Without removing his eyes from her face, he reached for his fly and said, "War wounds."

She studied the lines fanning out from his lashes, the groove along his cheek, the etchings bracketing his mouth. He had to be in his mid to late thirties. She wondered which war he wanted her to believe he'd fought.

"Desert Storm," he said, and undid his fly.

The grating sound of the parting zipper might as well have been nails dragging down a chalkboard. Her annoyance couldn't have been greater. This man read her far too easily. She'd learned to keep her emotions under such a tight wrap, most people found her impenetrable. She liked it that way.

"I haven't got all night," she said, and picked up the Glock to check if it was loaded. It was...less one bullet.

"You can look now."

She blinked and transferred her attention from the chamber to Travis. He'd dropped his jeans and stood only in black silk boxers. Which hid absolutely nothing.

"Satisfied?"

At the mocking tone of his voice, she clenched her jaw. Deliberately, she let her gaze drift across his chest, to the bulge of his left bicep, then trail down his stomach to linger on the fullness beneath his shorts.

Her breath bunched and expanded in her throat. It had been a long time since she'd been with a man. Too long, obviously. Slowly, carefully, she exhaled and continued her perusal, noting the ridge of muscles cording the length of his thighs, his equally well-developed calves. He was a runner. Or some type of athlete. Or maybe dodging bullets put him in such good shape. The sobering thought chased away her feminine appreciation, replacing it with caution.

"You're okay." She picked up the shirt he'd laid aside and threw it at him with a little too much force.

"Am I?" He made a one-handed catch. "I can take off the shorts if you want."

"Look, Travis, I don't like you and I don't like your tone. So skip the baiting and state your business."

His mouth curved in a satisfied smile as he abandoned the shirt and pulled up his jeans. It was then she noticed the cowboy boots he wore. A small .22 caliber *could* fit in there.

"Now what?" The snap of his fly brought her gaze level with his. Impatience had replaced amusement in his dark eyes.

She stared back with purpose. "I told you to state your business."

He jerked on his shirt. "I need to find someone."

When he didn't elaborate, she arched a brow. "That much I figured out."

He ignored her sarcasm. "His name is Dylan Sands. He has an inheritance coming to him, but we can't find him."

She frowned. "Why would you come to a bounty hunter? Finding someone is simple enough."

"There are extenuating circumstances...." He paused, studying her in a way that stirred her unease. "When do I talk to Scott?"

Taryn straightened. His question caught her off guard. So did his sudden take-charge tone. "When I decide if this case is feasible."

He let a few moments of silence stretch, his gaze becoming more insolent, more smug. "How often does this act work?"

"What act?"

"Come on. You're no go-between."

"Look, if you want to talk to Scott, you'll have—"

"You're more than a girlfriend. Maybe..." His eyes narrowed with suspicion...disbelief. "You can't be Scott."

She laughed. "That's some leap."

Slowly he shook his head, his forehead wrinkling. For the first time, he looked a little unsure. "I seem to remember talk of a partner." His frown deepened. "You?"

She shrugged off his obvious skepticism…the trace of disappointment. The hell with him. She didn't care if he knew she'd been the brains behind the operation. "Gee, you caught me."

"Where's Scott?"

He startled her with his sudden sharpness, made her want to recant her admission. "Dead," she said, with a bluntness that further surprised her.

"Dead?" He reared back in amazement. "When?"

"About a year ago."

He drew a hand down his face, covering his mouth for a moment. "Damn," he said, the sound muffled, frustrated.

Taryn watched with interest as the lines deepened across his forehead and flecks of irritation gleamed in his dark eyes. For whatever reason, hiring Derek specifically was important to him. Or maybe Scott Investigations' eighty-eight percent retrieval rate was what attracted him. If so, she was still here, able-bodied, willing to go after a bounty for the right price. And he claimed to have some major cash to spend.

"Tell me more about the case," she said, and he blinked, then stared at her as if he'd forgotten she was here.

"Isn't it a moot point now?" he asked.

"Not necessarily. If the case is legitimate, I'll still consider taking it." Although why his client would be willing to pay big bucks for what seemed like a half-day, no-brainer investigation she couldn't figure.

"By yourself?"

Of all the things she imagined this guy to be, a sexist wasn't one of them. She folded her arms across her chest, leaned back and stared at him. "Why, yes, all by my lonesome," she said with exaggerated sweetness, and then her amusement slid away and she narrowed her gaze. "Unless you're not being straight with me. You said something about extenuating circumstances?"

Travis didn't hurry to respond. He picked up his jacket and pulled it on. Then he started to reach for his gun, paused and said, "May I?"

She gave him a curt nod. She wasn't certain she wanted the case. Something didn't smell right. But she sure as hell wasn't going to let him dismiss her out of hand, either. Besides, he hadn't told her how much money he was willing to pay yet.

After he tucked the gun into the waistband of his jeans, he pocketed the knife. "Sands is an importer...mostly high-end artifacts from the Middle East and Africa. Does most of his business with rich collectors. He has an apartment near the Galleria and an office off Westheimer."

Taryn frowned. If Travis already knew all this... "Ever thought of knocking on his door?"

"Ah, you have a sense of humor. Good." He reached into his breast pocket and withdrew a flat leather case. "You'll need one. Sands has been missing for nearly a year."

"As in he went to the corner for bread and never came home?"

"Something like that. He went on vacation...a Caribbean cruise. The ship docked in Jamaica. Sands got off, just like half the people on the ship, but he never got back on."

She cut loose a long, slow breath to counter the sudden rush of adrenaline starting to pump through her veins. This was her kind of case—meaty... intriguing. It should pay a lot, too. Carefully masking her excitement, she shook her head and pursed her lips in a show of reluctance. "A trail gets awfully cold in a year."

"Now you understand why I need the best."

"That would be me."

Nick Travis's mouth curved in an unreadable smile.

Taryn wasn't sure she liked this man. One minute she did and the next she wanted nothing more than to send him flying against the wall. More important, she still wasn't sure if she trusted him. "The best doesn't come cheap," she said, eyeing the small leather case he'd withdrawn.

"Nor should it," he agreed, and slipped out a wad of crisp new bills. Thousand-dollar ones. Lots of them. He had to be holding fifty grand in his hand. Probably more.

"Those real?" Stupid question, but her heart was racing and she needed a moment to think.

"I'm a busy man." He fanned the bills out on the pool table. "I don't play games."

She dragged her gaze away from the money...money that would go a long way toward buying her and Lucy a new life. When her eyes met his, she saw a flash of doubt and realized he hadn't decided yet if he wanted to hire her.

His reluctance reassured her. She still didn't trust him, but she no longer felt targeted, either. A few phone calls and she'd confirm his identity, and if he'd lied about the Sands case, she'd find that out, too.

She stepped away from the table, smoothed down her skirt and forbade herself from even so much as glancing at the money again.

"Tomorrow evening," she told him, "I'll call you at seven and let you know if I'll take the case."

He met her bluff with a speculative frown that darkened his eyes and gave his mouth a sensual twist. He could tell her to go to hell, but something told her he wouldn't. Unfortunately, that same something warned her she was getting in over her head.

"I haven't told you where I'm staying," he said finally.

Taryn smiled. "No, you haven't," she said before heading for the door. "Seven. Be there."

Chapter Two

Nick Travis exited the cab in front of Myron's Place and checked his watch. Six-fifty-five. She should be here, probably about ready to call him at his hotel. He had no doubt she had checked him out and tracked him down. The woman possessed a confidence that assured him she was competent.

As soon as she'd picked up the Glock last night he'd known she was no flunky or some man's trophy. She knew what she was doing. She was cautious, too, and he liked cautious. A reckless investigation could ruin his plans. Too bad she was so damn beautiful. In his experience, that spelled trouble.

He opened the door and saw her immediately. She'd be hard to miss, sitting at the bar, her long, shiny hair hanging down her back like a swatch of fine pale silk. Tonight she wore jeans, faded, tight, hugging her slim waist and molding her fanny into a heart shape perched on the stool as she was. Pity about the jeans. She had killer legs.

Except Nick wasn't here to admire her generous curves, or appreciate the fire in her blue eyes. He needed someone capable, thorough and if necessary, lethal. From his digging around today, he knew she fit the bill. That's why he was going to hire her. He refused to go out with another life on his conscience.

The clack of balls subsided and the two Neanderthal types leaning over the pool table straightened to give him ominous looks. Several more heads turned toward him and the noise level lowered a couple more decibels. Taryn glanced over her shoulder.

Surprise, then annoyance flashed in her eyes before her face went blank and she swiveled around on the stool to face him. Quite a display of emotion, coming from the ice queen. She liked operating on her own terms, obviously needed the control. No tipping her cards. That much was made clear last night. Her vigilance encouraged him. It could keep them both alive.

"I told you I'd call," she said, and he saw the antiquated black rotary phone sitting in front of her.

He glanced at his watch, then took a seat beside her. "You're prompt. I like that."

"*You* can't follow instructions worth a damn."

He shrugged. "I'm used to giving them."

"That's about to change."

He smiled as he watched Taryn pick up her mug of beer and take a sip, then he signaled the bartender to give him the same. The big bruiser who'd taken Nick's fifty last night grunted something that sounded like a laugh and pulled out a cloudy-looking mug.

Nick turned back to Taryn. "You find out everything you need to know?"

"What's the capital of Idaho?"

He frowned until he figured out where she was headed. She'd done a thorough job of checking him out, his own sources had substantiated that, and yet she still looked for confirmation. "I doubt everyone knows the capital of the state they live in."

"I bet you do." Her gaze locked with his, challenge sparkling in her blue eyes. What did she think—if he wasn't who he'd said he was, that he'd suddenly spill a confession?

The bartender set a mug in front of Nick, and he used the brief distraction to study Taryn. This woman fascinated him. She still didn't trust him, was apparently suspicious of his identity, yet she wanted this case, despite her pretense to the contrary. But something was making her edgy, so why take it at all?

The money, of course. That's why he'd offered so much. For most people, cash was a powerful motivator, the hell with fear. Or principle.

"Tell me something," he said, wrapping his hand around the mug in front of him. "Why the paranoia?"

A startled laugh breached her full pink lips, curving them, diminishing his good sense to lust. "What makes you ask?"

"Do you grill all your clients?" he asked. "Or make them strip?"

She blinked. "I already *know* all my other clients. They don't come walking in here off the street. By the way, how did you hear about Scott Investigations?"

"Another attorney. Sam Jones, I think. But that was about a year ago." He watched her eyebrows furrow as she processed the information. "That's why I didn't know about your husband's death. I'm sorry."

She straightened, her chin lifting ever so slightly. "But you do now."

"You weren't the only one doing your homework today, Mrs. Scott."

On the bar beside her hand lay two straws, one of

them knotted and misshapen. The other one she clamped between her fingers in a desperate way that told him she'd once been a smoker, and that she'd give just about anything for a cigarette right now.

"My husband was often reckless. It ultimately got him killed. Now maybe you understand my caution."

"Did it happen on the job?"

The straw dropped to the bar. She shoved her hand through her hair, letting the pale strands fall around her shoulders and trail her bare arms. Her red T-shirt was sleeveless, showing off skin that was golden and well-toned. "I don't want to talk about Derek."

Nick nodded and thoughtfully raised the beer to his lips. He hadn't meant to upset her. Though obviously not the grieving widow, clearly she was still at odds with Scott's death. He took a sip, then frowned at the amber liquid. "This isn't—What is this?"

"Ginger ale, I expect." Amusement softened her features, lightened the usual steeliness in her eyes. The right side of her mouth twitched. The overall effect was devastating. She shrugged. "I don't drink when I'm working."

"So you decided to take the case."

Her face was a mask again, all business. "On two conditions. You've got to be totally straight with me. If I find out otherwise, I'm out, no matter how close I am to finding Sands. And you forfeit any money already paid me."

"Okay," he said slowly. "The second condition?"

"Once I find him, it's up to Sands if I reveal his whereabouts."

"And if he wants to…say…stay lost?"

"That's his prerogative, Mr. Travis. You'll have

wasted some time and your client will be out a few bucks. But that's the deal.''

''Call me a simple country boy, but the amount my client is willing to pay hardly seems like just *a few bucks.*''

The cynicism that briefly lifted one side of her mouth at the country boy reference was quickly replaced with a look of firm resolve that set her jaw firm and locked her gaze with his. ''If you and your client are on the up and up, then all this won't matter, will it? Who's going to turn down an inheritance?''

''I certainly wouldn't. But then again, I have nothing to hide.''

''Everyone has a skeleton or two in the closet, Mr. Travis. For your sake, I hope none of yours have anything to do with this case.''

Nick smiled and toyed with his mug. ''Would, say, another ten thousand buy a certain amount of discretion?''

She stiffened. ''You know my terms.''

''Fifteen thousand?''

''Forget it.'' She started to slide off the bar stool.

He laid a restraining hand on her arm. ''Relax, Taryn. I agree to your terms. I shouldn't have baited you.''

She hesitated, but her sudden move off the stool had drawn several threatening looks. He had the feeling all she had to do was blink and half the bar's occupants would gladly cram their fists down his throat. A wise man would unhand her.

But a pulse fluttered wildly at her wrist beneath skin that was warm and incredibly soft. Much softer than he'd imagined as he'd lain awake last night calling himself a fool for considering hiring her.

Long blond strands of hair clung to her arm. Almost within his reach. His sudden, insane desire to explore its softness shocked him back to his senses. He didn't have to look around to know that at least a dozen pairs of angry eyes targeted him. He met her blue steely ones, only inches from his own. The simmering challenge he found there told him to back off.

Hell, he hadn't come this far to commit suicide in some Houston dive. Releasing her, he relaxed in his seat. She edged back onto her stool, the action slow, calculated.

She'd been ready to walk away from the deal...from the money. No doubt about it. Nick had to admire her conviction. It was damn refreshing. Maybe he should let her go. She was too much of a distraction.

And then again, maybe a distraction was just what he needed. All eyes would be on her. If he remembered where to keep his own, Taryn Scott could turn out to be his trump card.

The bartender had appeared again, his big meaty fist opening and closing as if it itched to plant itself in Nick's face. After shooting him a warning look, Taryn gave the guy a small jerk of her head, and with a disappointed grimace, he picked up an empty pitcher and headed back toward the other end of the bar.

She returned her attention to Nick. "Problem is, I don't trust you, Travis. I don't know if I can work for someone I don't trust."

"I'm a plain, garden-variety attorney, for God's sake. What's not to trust?"

A slow and grudging smile tugged at her mouth.

"I've already heard all the lawyer jokes," he said. "How can I ease your mind?"

"Tell me the truth."

"The truth?" He grunted to himself, then took a long, cool sip of ginger ale, letting it soothe the bitterness coating the inside of his mouth. "Maybe we're both being lied to, but I can only tell you what I know."

He set the mug down and stared at it, using the moment of pensive silence to banish his demons before he looked at her.

The distrustful gleam had been extinguished in her eyes, but brief uncertainty flared in its place. "Tell me this case has nothing to do with blackmail or embezzlement or revenge."

His genuine surprise at her suspicion apparently showed because when he shook his head, relief eased the tension around her mouth. "I give you my word on that. If you find Sands, no harm will come to him." Certainly not by Nick's hands, anyway. "If he tells you he doesn't want to be found, I disappear. No problem."

She straightened, nodded. "Okay. Looks like we have a deal, Mr. Travis."

"If we're going to be working together, it'll be easier if you call me Nick."

She'd started to extend her hand. Now she pulled it back. "Working together?"

He shrugged, cursing to himself when defensiveness brought renewed doubt to her expression. "Just a figure of speech," he said casually.

"I work alone."

"Of course."

"You *do* understand?"

"Sure. I'm an attorney. What do I know about a missing person investigation?"

"Exactly."

He gave her a reassuring smile.

She responded with a silent, cold, assessing stare.

"Deal?" he asked, offering his hand.

She dragged her gaze from his face long enough to glance at his palm, making no move to respond further. "Half the money up front. The other half on delivery."

He nodded, then withdrew his hand when he realized all she wanted from him was her fee. And his word. "Anything else?"

"That should cover it."

This time when she extended her hand, he didn't make the same mistake. He slipped a thick cream-colored envelope out of his pocket and laid it across her palm. Her eyebrows rose in question, presumably reacting to his preparedness, and he said, "There's an extra thousand there."

She didn't count it, just lifted her shirt high enough to shove the envelope into the waistband of her jeans.

And long enough for him to get a glimpse of firm golden skin, a ridge of well-defined muscle.

He wanted to see her naked.

The sudden thought ambushed him, splintered his control as easily as a hatchet split a log into kindling. He released a long, slow breath. In his pocket, his cell phone rang and he grabbed for it, glad for the distraction.

He knew who was calling, and no way could he have this conversation in front of Taryn. Good thing. He needed some air. "Excuse me," he said, and she nodded as she continued to rearrange her shirt over the envelope.

He'd made it halfway to the door when it occurred to him that he'd just given her a huge sum of cash in front of a school of bottom-feeders. Hesitating near the door, he answered the call, his gaze carefully circling the room.

Bent over the pool table, two of the meanest sons of bitches he'd ever seen were lining up shots. The rest of the crowd were either gulping beer from pitchers, or passing joints, but no one seemed to be paying him or Taryn any attention.

"Travis?"

The caller's voice came across the line a second time, this attempt more anxious, and raspy.

"Yeah, I'm here," Nick said, his gaze drawing again to Taryn. He needed to worry about her about as much as he needed another .22 caliber slug in his gut. Judging by the excellent shape she was in, she could probably drop him a time or two. Besides, this feral crowd seemed to take care of their own.

Except a blind man could see Taryn wasn't one of them, he thought, giving the occupants a final glance before stepping out into the privacy of the darkened street. And that contradiction made him more curious than was sensible.

"Travis? What the hell is going on?"

"We just cut the deal," Nick said. "She's on the case."

"Good." His boss coughed away from the phone but the racking sound still tore through Nick. Thirty-five years of heavy smoking had finally caught up with the old man. "She'd better get on it right away.

I'd like to see this case wrapped up before they use me as fertilizer.''

Nick winced at the man's blunt acceptance. ''I know,'' he said quietly. ''But she's good. She'll get the job done quickly.''

''I'm counting on that. I know you are, too.''

''Yeah.'' Nick rubbed the side of his lightly stubbled jaw with a weary hand. He'd waited a long time for this. Too long.

''She gonna start looking for Sands tomorrow?''

''I'd expect so.'' From what he'd learned about her, Nick was guessing she'd already started. ''Let's just hope she doesn't find him.''

Chapter Three

After spending a disappointing morning at her computer, Taryn choked down lunch on the way to Dylan Sands's office. The greasy hot dog didn't sit well with her, or maybe it was that persistent uneasy feeling that was making her a little queasy.

Everything about the man checked out like a connect-the-dot child's game. His background was so pat, so accessible, it was almost as if it were designed. Up until the day he disappeared. The whole thing stunk. It spelled witness protection.

One of her sources knew a customs agent who dealt with Sands and was able to provide information on some interesting personal habits. Unfortunately, nothing she'd learned was helpful. Yet.

The information Travis had given her hadn't panned out. Which didn't surprise her. She figured he'd already checked out the list of names, numbers and businesses Sands used. Even though Travis claimed he'd only called Sands's place of employment, he didn't strike her as a passive man and she didn't believe for one minute he hadn't done his own checking. Maybe he hadn't liked what he found.

Maybe he was setting her up.

She exhaled a curse as she pulled into the parking garage adjoining Sands's office building. One more day. Then she'd decide if she should bow out. By then she'd have exhausted all her sources. So far, no one knew anything about a man with Sands's description being in the protection program. Not that that was a safe bet. Her sources were good. Not foolproof. And no way was she getting mixed up in a revenge or mob hit.

Then, too, she hadn't discounted the paranoia that had plagued her since Derek's death. If something didn't break soon, her butt would end up on a shrink's couch. For Lucy's sake. Her daughter deserved a mother with all her marbles.

The elevator ride was short, taking her to Cain's Imports, a modest office on the fourth floor that didn't even have a reception desk. Sands's impressive salary and snazzy condo address had brought another picture to mind.

A scraping noise came from behind an Oriental design screen, and then a gruff male voice asked, "Can I help you?"

A short man with thinning brown hair rounded the partition and peered over his reading glasses at her. Wariness lined his forehead. Age hunched his narrow shoulders.

She gave him a smile, the one that got her in most doors, and extended her business card. "I'm Taryn Scott of Scott Investigations. I have a few questions about an ex-employee. Dylan Sands."

The man had just taken the card, but at the mention of Sands, it slipped from his hand and fluttered to the drab green carpet. He stared at her, stunned, alarm beginning to draw his brows together, while he made no move to retrieve the card.

She stooped to pick it up and noticed another pair of shoes underneath the partition. But no one made a sound on the other side.

She smiled again when she returned the card to him.

The man accepted it with an unsteady hand. "Sands? He disappeared about a year ago. Some fellow just asked about him last week." Folding his arms across his chest, he narrowed his eyes and gave her the once-over. "What do you want to know about Sands?"

"I didn't catch your name."

He stared at her for a long silent moment. "Cross. Richard Cross."

"And you are—?" She turned up the wattage of her smile. "His boss?"

"That would be the owner, Harrison Cain. I'm Mr. Cain's assistant."

"I see. Maybe I could speak with him after we talk?"

Cross frowned. "You haven't told me what you wanted to know about Sands. Who are you working for, anyway?"

"I'm sure you know I can't tell you that," she said in a teasing voice she used to get what she wanted. The cutesiness made her want to puke. "But I can say that Mr. Sands will be a very rich man once I find him."

"It can't be an inheritance. Both his parents are dead. He didn't have any other family."

She shrugged. "Someone left him something."

Cross rubbed his clean-shaven jaw, his pale blue

eyes studying her intensely. "You aren't going to find any new information here. The police combed his desk and took all his personal things. They didn't find anything." He shrugged. "If you ask me, Sands had a mess of cash stashed away in a Cayman account. No one's going to see that guy again."

Taryn glanced around the cramped office. The copy and fax machines were old, the pair of desks and chairs shabby. Only the three computers sitting near the dirty window were state-of-the-art models. Not exactly a prosperous-looking business. Anyway, embezzlement hadn't been suspected of Sands. She'd checked.

"I hadn't heard that theory yet," she said in a sugary voice, the tilt of her head coy. "What makes you say that?"

Cross hesitated, the wariness entering his eyes again. Then he shrugged, and by his guarded expression she knew she wouldn't get anything more out of him. "They didn't find the body. He's gotta be somewhere. And he can't be living on air."

She needed another tactic. "You didn't like Mr. Sands, did you?"

"He was okay. A little arrogant. But the young ones often are."

"The young ones?"

Cross shifted his weight, a dull red climbing his neck. "I'm busy, and I obviously can't help you, Ms. Scott." Gesturing toward the door, he took a step in that direction. "So if you'll excuse me…"

"Isn't there someone else I can speak with? You mentioned your boss. Mr. Cain, is it?"

"He's not here. He has a doctor's appointment."

"Maybe I could come back another time. Later this afternoon, perhaps?"

Cross shook his head. "Not today. He rarely comes back after his appointments. But he could probably see you tomorrow morning. I think his schedule is open."

His sudden accommodating manner surprised Taryn. However, he still failed to mention the person on the other side of the partition. "I'll be here any time you say."

"Let me check his day planner."

"Are you the only two people working in this office?" she called out as Cross disappeared behind the partition, her gaze quickly scanning the room for anything of interest.

"We have two independent importers who work out of here when they aren't on the road. That would be Dennis Maynard and Syd Sebastian."

One of the machines started whirring and she repositioned herself to get a glimpse of an incoming fax. Within an instant, Cross reappeared, his gaze darting from the fax machine to Taryn. He smiled, but his eyes issued a warning. "Tomorrow at ten should be all right."

"Any chance I'll be able to speak to the other two?" She nonchalantly looked past the fax out the window, as if that was where her interest lay.

"Possibly. Though there's no telling when either of them will come by. I don't usually know when they're in town."

The words were barely out of his mouth when the door opened and they both turned to find a stocky, dark-haired man in his mid-thirties entering the office. He looked like a jock.

''Seems you're in luck,'' Cross said, without enthusiasm. ''Meet Syd Sebastian.''

The younger man gave her a brief once-over, then smiled. ''You looking for me? My alimony check went out yesterday.''

''I'm sure your ex-wife would be glad to hear that.'' Taryn handed him her business card. ''I only want to know about Dylan Sands.''

Syd reared back his head in frank surprise. ''Dylan? I figured everybody gave up on him by now.''

''I tried to tell her that,'' Cross said.

Sebastian sent the man a none-too-friendly sidelong glance. ''I turned my expense account in yesterday, and I'm sure I forgot to cross a few t's. Why don't you go nitpick it?''

Cross gave him a look of pure disdain. ''Don't forget you have an appointment in half an hour. You can't be late.''

Taryn remained expressionless as the two men exchanged dark looks. So Richard Cross had known Sebastian was in town. ''I only have a couple of questions. If you don't mind, I'd be happy to ride with you to your appointment.''

Sebastian's affability slipped. ''That's not possible. We can talk while I pull a few things together.'' He preceded her to the desk closest to the window.

''Which one was Sands's desk?'' she asked, looking freely around now that Cross had disappeared behind the partition again, and Sebastian was busy rifling through drawers.

''Gone.''

''The entire desk?''

He nodded absently while frowning at an open file folder. ''What the hell did I do with that printout?''

"You didn't like Sands."

He brought his head up and met her gaze. "Hell, yeah, I liked him. We played squash every Saturday we were both in town. He was probably the closest person I had to a friend."

Another surprise. "I'm sorry. You seem so..."

"Indifferent?" He shook his head and started flipping through file folders again. "Resigned is more like it. One of two things happened. Either he was murdered or he doesn't want to be found. And if Dylan doesn't want to be found, he won't be."

"Murdered?"

He shrugged, but the casual gesture didn't fool her. Wariness darkened his already-black eyes. "He was a sharply dressed American tourist. Maybe one of the local bad guys thought he had a lot of cash."

"And if he simply disappeared? Why would he want to do that?"

Sebastian gave her a long, measuring look, then glanced at her card again. "What's all this about?"

She smiled patiently and gave him the same canned speech she'd given Richard Cross. If Sebastian didn't believe her, she couldn't tell. His expression was totally blank as he finished loading his briefcase.

"Look," he said, making a move for the door. "I'd really like to help you out, but I don't have any information that hasn't already been checked and double-checked. And right now I have an appointment that can't wait."

"Maybe we could talk again tomorrow," Taryn said, walking him toward the elevator. "I have an appointment with Mr. Cain at ten. After, I'll spring for lunch. You choose the restaurant."

He shook his head. "No can do. I have a plane to

catch at one.'' After punching the elevator button, he turned to her with his lips stretched over a set of snow-white teeth, his gaze roaming her face. "I'll be back in a week. Let's make that dinner.''

She forced a smile. Sebastian had more than his share of charm. But she wasn't interested. Men had made her life complicated since she was old enough to date. Besides, she hoped to have the case wrapped up inside of a week.

"Maybe I'll give you a call," she said, and judging by the cocky wink he gave her, she pretty much figured most women didn't disappoint him. This time he'd better not hold his breath.

The car to the elevator opened. He got in and held the door. "Coming down?"

"I think I'll see who else in the office is available to talk to me."

"No one else is in there but Cross. And he hasn't had anything worthwhile to say in twenty years."

She chuckled. "You go ahead. I need to duck into the rest room.''

As soon as the doors closed, she lost the smile. Wrong answer. There was someone else in that office. Did Sebastian know? Was he just giving her the same song and dance as Cross?

She didn't return, knowing nothing would be accomplished there today, and took the next elevator. She still had Sands's apartment to check out. Tomorrow she hoped to get more information from Harrison Cain.

The drive to the apartment was short, but parking was a problem. The entire ten minutes it took her to find a spot, her skin prickled with the sense of being watched. As soon as she got out of the car, she knew why.

"Travis, what the hell are you doing here?" She slammed the door and watched him cross the street. A red Porsche missed him by a foot. Too bad.

"What did you find out?" He jogged the last couple of yards.

"You followed me."

He shrugged. "No harm, no foul."

"Wrong. Next time you so blatantly violate our agreement, I'm off the case." She stuck a couple of quarters in the meter and started at a brisk pace toward the apartment building.

"Hold on." He hurried to catch up, his shoulder brushing hers as he matched her stride.

She stopped, abruptly facing him. "I told you I'd see you tonight. Go back to your hotel."

"Working together makes more sense. I might think of something to ask that you missed."

"We had this discussion already, Travis," she said, her voice tight. "I work alone. Or I don't work for you at all."

He had on dark glasses even though it was an overcast day, and she couldn't see his eyes. But she felt them on her. Assessing her. Trying to unravel her. She wouldn't let him.

"So far, I haven't found any evidence that he's surfaced in the last year. He hasn't used his social security number or his driver's license or his bank cards. I suggest you go back to your hotel. I'll call you as soon as I get done here. Maybe then I'll have something to report."

He slowly brought a hand up to stroke his jaw. He hadn't shaved yet. It made him all the more attractive...dangerous. Just her type. Dammit. "Didn't you find anything out at his office?"

"Look, I'm trying to be patient. Cooperative, even. Now, beat it." Irritation had slipped into her voice, but it didn't seem to faze him. Not so much as a twitch betrayed his thoughts.

Then his hardened expression relaxed, and a slow, sheepish smile spread across his face. "Okay, I'll admit it. I'm kind of a groupie. Investigative work fascinates me." He shrugged. "That's why I wanted to tag along."

Right. And she was Elvis reincarnated. "I'm not sure how I'm going to enter Sands's apartment. And if I have to break in, I don't want you involved."

Disappointment swiftly replaced his grin. It almost seemed genuine. He was damned good. She'd give him that. "I guess I shouldn't be a witness to anything illegal. Unless you need someone to watch your back."

He'd be watching more than her back, she'd bet. She shook her head. "Technically, as a bounty hunter, I can legally enter. Except Sands doesn't have a bounty on his head, so I'm stretching it here. But you wouldn't be exempt." Her lips curved in feminine persuasion. Two could play this game. "So why don't you go on back to the hotel? I'll call as soon as I leave here."

He didn't answer for a minute, and all she could see was her own impatient reflection in the dark lenses of his glasses. And the sensual shape of his mouth as it started to lift hypnotically at the corners.

"You're really pretty when you smile," he said finally, his voice lowering.

Taryn stiffened. "I'll see you later." She swung toward the apartment entrance.

"I'll wait in the lobby," he called out before she made it through the double glass doors.

She didn't argue, didn't so much as give him a glance. She smiled at the doorman as if she had every right to be there and headed straight for the elevators, jabbing the call button so hard that her finger bent back. She let out a succinct curse. Why the hell was she letting him get to her like this?

If she hadn't already decided to get out of the business, this case would be the last straw. She was losing her edge. For a split second, she'd actually been flattered.

Flattered.

How incredibly stupid! He'd only meant to distract her. And even if he hadn't, she needed to keep her eye on the ball. The sooner she wrapped up this case, the sooner she and Lucy could start their new life.

The bell dinged the elevator's arrival and Taryn blinked, finally taking note of her surroundings. She'd easily recognized the uptown address of the condo, but the cylinder-shaped building was even more posh than she'd expected. How could someone like Sands afford digs like this? He couldn't make that much money as an importer. Not legally, anyway.

Maybe his disappearance was a result of a smuggling deal gone bad. Yet he had a squeaky-clean record. Not so much as an outstanding parking ticket that she could find. Although she knew that didn't necessarily mean anything. Only that if he had been crooked, he was also careful.

Sands's floor was just below the penthouse and was shared by only one other unit. She saw his door to the right as soon as she got off the elevator. No sign of his neighbor's door. It was probably on the other side. Good. She already knew she'd have to break in. Better there'd be no witnesses.

Just as a precaution, she strolled down the opposite corridor that curved to the left, until she came to the other door, numbered one-o-two. Unlike the barrenness of Sands's door, this one was decorated with a wreath of fresh herbs and flowers. In the middle was a hand-painted sign that read Welcome.

Taryn continued past and found only solitude and a stairway exit before arriving at Sands's door again. For the hell of it, she knocked, waited a moment, then jiggled the doorknob. It was locked.

No surprise. No more than the fact that the apartment had been paid up and kept in Sands's name for more than a year. That was the biggest puzzle she hadn't been able to piece together. Why would a man pay his lease eighteen months in advance if he'd intended to disappear? In fact, why would he tie his money up like that at all?

Taryn didn't have too much of a head for business, but that didn't make sense even to her. And Sands couldn't afford a place like this if he was a bad businessman. Which left the possibility that someone else had paid up the lease. But who? And why?

After another cautious glance over her shoulder, she withdrew a small leather case from her purse and proceeded to unlock the door. It was a quality lock and it took her a little longer than usual, but the latch finally gave and she gingerly pushed the door open.

The sweet scent of jasmine drifted toward her, instead of the musty dankness she'd expected. The living room drapes were open, letting in the murky light of the overcast skies. Artfully arranged antiques and African artifacts made the room more chic than cozy.

She took a step over the threshold and discovered the source of the surprising flowery scent. On a side table, two lush plants sat in blue Oriental pots, their leaves and blooms cascading nearly to the floor.

She moved toward them, but heard something behind her. Before she could turn around, a barrel of a gun poked the small of her back.

Chapter Four

Taryn froze. She cleared her throat, then started to turn around.

"Don't move."

The voice was slightly high. Scared. The gun shook. Not a good thing.

"I won't move until you say it's okay," Taryn said in a calm, soothing tone. "But I would like to turn around."

"No." The gun dug deeper, and Taryn flinched. "Tell me what you're doing here," the voice said. It belonged to a man, an elderly one.

"I'm a friend of Dylan's."

"I've never seen you before."

"I, uh, usually visited him late at night." She faked a small embarrassed shrug of one shoulder, and hoped he caught her implication. Remembering the wreath, she tried another bluff. "Are you his neighbor? The one who loves flowers?"

The gun slackened against her back. "He spoke of me?"

"Yes. Very fondly."

After a brief silence, his voice quivering slightly, he asked, "What's your name?"

"Taryn. Taryn Scott. May I turn around now?"

"And what did you say you were doing here?"

"I came to pick up some things I'd left. I figured there wouldn't be any harm. You know, since it doesn't look like Dylan will be coming back."

The pressure of the gun eased. "He'll be back. You mark my words, young lady. He'll be back." Conviction strengthened his voice, made him sound a little angry.

Slowly she began to turn around. He made no move to stop her, and when she finally faced him, she saw the cane in his hand. No gun. Just the cane. Shaking her head, she lowered her arms and stared into faded gray eyes level with hers.

He cast a sheepish glance at the cane, then met her gaze again. "You can't be too careful these days," he said, then his white brows drew together to form two wary creases. "Besides, I didn't hear you knock."

She doubted he would have, but shrugged. "I did. Not that I thought anyone would answer."

He frowned at the inference, his face remarkably unlined in contrast to his shock of white hair. "I didn't hear you. I was in my greenhouse, but I usually try to listen for any visitors."

She smiled and put out her hand. "I'm sorry, I don't remember your name."

"Archibald Hanes, madam, and it's a pleasure to make your acquaintance." He took her hand and brushed it with his lips.

The sudden transformation to perfect gentleman was encouraging. "Likewise, Mr. Hanes."

"Could I offer you some tea?"

Taryn hesitated. She'd rather he leave her in

Sands's apartment. She left her hand in his a second longer, then withdrew it. "I'd love some."

"Excellent." He motioned her into the hall, then pulled Sands's door closed. The lock clicked. "I have several varieties, of course. Afternoon tea is so civilized, don't you think? That's one of my favorite things about England."

She nodded and walked ahead of him with a furtive glance at her watch. She hoped he had something useful to tell her, although she doubted it. But if she wanted to get into Sands's apartment, she wasn't going to do it by alienating this guy.

Within a half hour, her suspicion was confirmed. Despite her subtle probing, Archibald Hanes, retired for fourteen years, widowed for twelve, Dylan's neighbor for ten, didn't have a damn bit of significant information for her, only a deep affection for the man who'd disappeared a year ago.

"Have you ever seen this variety before?" Hanes asked, holding up a pot of mauve-colored orchids as he stepped back into the modestly decorated living room from the terrace greenhouse. "Dylan and I had a bet once that I couldn't grow it here in Houston. I got the whole inside of my apartment painted as a result of that particular wager." His chuckle faded. "Although I suspect that was Dylan's way of disguising his charity."

Taryn's gaze switched from her watch to his face and she straightened slightly. "Yup, that wouldn't surprise me. He was certainly that kind of guy," she said, and saw surprise briefly flicker in the old man's eyes. "I mean, he was caring like that." She was blowing it. Her research had painted a different picture of the man. A loner. Arrogant. Self-absorbed.

"Sometimes." She shrugged. "But you know how he could be when he was in one of his moods."

Archibald laughed. "You don't have to try and soft-pedal around me. Dylan is like the son I never had. I know that boy inside and out. And God knows he has his faults." His amusement dwindled. "But he's been extremely kind to this old man, and no one can argue with that."

She settled back in her chair, the contradictions colliding in her head. From everything Hanes had told her about himself, she wondered how he could afford this luxury apartment. Had Sands been subsidizing him? The idea didn't jive with what she already knew. At this rate, she was never going to get a handle on the kind of man Sands was.

Another thing that intrigued her was how Hanes continued to speak of Dylan in the present tense. She herself wasn't so hopeful. Maybe she was wrong in posing as a bed partner. This man obviously cared a great deal about Sands and believed he was coming back. Maybe she'd get further by telling him the truth, that Sands stood to gain a substantial inheritance. At this point it wouldn't hurt. She needed to get into that apartment. Legally would be better. And she figured Hanes had a key.

"Would you like to see what I've done with the place?" Archibald asked absently, his attention channeled toward a critical inspection of his plant. "I think I may take this little one over for a while. It loves Dylan's morning sun."

She tried not to look too eager when she realized what he meant. "You've been keeping things up for him? How nice."

"I wouldn't want him to come home to an apartment full of dust and cobwebs. Besides, I have to water his plants.'' He moved to the door and stopped. ''Are you coming?''

She left her chair and the untouched tea and followed him out the door, noticing that he never stopped to pick up a key. But when they arrived at Dylan's apartment, he promptly produced one and let them both in.

As she walked past the foyer and was allowed a more unhurried look, she was struck by how immaculate the place was. And lived-in. As though Sands had left only yesterday. Except for the piles of magazines and numerous stacks of mail.

''Look how splendid Samantha looks,'' Archibald said, and Taryn's gaze immediately flew toward the door. ''It's that morning sun, I tell you. They all love it.''

No one was there, of course. She realized he was talking about the cascading yellow orchid he held up. Smiling a little, she gently touched the delicate petals. ''She is a beauty.''

Hanes beamed, and Taryn felt a small tug at her heart. Was this what it was going to be like to grow old, alone? She pushed away the cloying sentimentality. Even if Derek had lived, she would have been alone. And there was nothing worse than living with someone who inspired such aching loneliness that you wondered why you bothered getting out of bed in the morning.

The old man's pleased smile gave way to a considering frown, and then he cocked his head to the side. ''Is that my phone?''

Hearing nothing, she started to shrug. ''Uh, I think it may be. You can probably still get it.''

''It's so hard to hear from here even with the ringer turned up.'' He had already headed for the door. ''I'll be right back.''

As soon as he disappeared, Taryn grabbed a stack of mail and shoved it into her purse. On the black marble kitchen counter was a notepad with something scribbled on it and she snatched that, too. Out of the corner of her eye, she saw the answering machine light blinking. Strange. How recently could that message have been left? She reached to depress the play button but heard something behind her.

She straightened just as Hanes walked back into the apartment, his cane thumping the tile foyer. ''My ears aren't what they used to be,'' he said, shaking his head. ''Or maybe they just hung up.''

If he wondered what she was doing in the kitchen, he didn't say anything. Just hobbled toward the row of plants sitting near the living room window.

''Look, Mr. Hanes, if it's all right with you, I'll just collect my things. I imagine they're, um, in the bedroom.'' She managed a sheepish look as his gaze met hers.

He looked at her a long time, his shoulders stooped as he relied heavily on the cane. But his eyes were alert. Measuring. Watchful. ''I don't think so.'' And then regret softened them. ''Dylan will surely be home any day now.''

She hesitated, wondering again if she'd be better off being straight with him. The trouble was, now he'd probably end up being more suspicious because she'd lied, and be totally uncooperative. ''May I leave you my number in case you change your mind?''

''You may, but I won't.'' He cleared his throat. ''I think you'd better leave your key with me.''

"My—?" She frowned. Of course he didn't know she'd picked the lock. "I don't have one. The door was open."

His white eyebrows drew sharply together. "That's impossible."

She smiled again as she scribbled her home number on a piece of scrap paper. "If I had my own key, I wouldn't be asking you to let me in, would I?"

He blinked as he accepted the slip of paper. "I suppose."

Damn, she wished she could listen to that phone message. In the far corner was an antique rolltop desk. She wouldn't mind rummaging through that, either. "Well, thank you for the tea."

His face brightened. "I could make you another cup."

"I really have to run. I still have some errands and there's rush hour traffic and all." A thought struck her. "Besides, tonight is *ER*. I have to get home in time for that."

He chuckled. "Past my bedtime, I'm afraid."

Perfect. She smiled again. "Goodbye, Mr. Hanes."

She would have felt sorry for the lonely old guy, except he eagerly transferred his attention to his orchids before she'd barely made it out the door.

She couldn't make it back tonight. There were three nights a week that were sacred to her. Nothing interfered with her scheduled visits with Lucy. Nothing. If Taryn didn't find anything interesting in the mail she'd swiped, she'd come back tomorrow night, after nine. When Hanes was asleep. She had a feeling not much got past the old man. Too much time on his hands, she supposed. Just like she'd have after Lucy was grown.

She stabbed the elevator button and stretched the tension building in her neck as she waited for the doors to slide open. What was up with all the maudlin thoughts lately? It wasn't like she wasn't used to being alone. In truth, she had been from the second year of her marriage to Derek. He'd been a loner, certainly not much of a husband. Or a friend. In fact, Derek hadn't been much good for anything. Except to scandalize her parents. And look where that display of rebellion had gotten her. Disowned. Lucy, too. That's what stung.

"What took you so long?"

Nick Travis started breathing down Taryn's neck the minute she left the elevator. She slid him a bland look and kept walking out into the fading twilight. It was still hot, making her skin grow moist. Of course in Houston, it was always hot and humid and sticky and she didn't know why the hell she hadn't just packed up and left. There was nothing here for her and Lucy. Except Derek's mother. But Olivia would follow her only granddaughter anywhere.

Of course, money was still a problem. It had been ever since Derek's death. In the wake of his lies. But after this case, she just might have enough to relocate them without plunging below poverty level.

Then all she had to do was figure out what to do with the rest of her life. A life without bounty hunting to pay the bills. She let out a pent-up breath. God, she hoped she wasn't as hopeless as Derek had called her. He'd told her how stupid she was often enough. Good thing she had looks, he'd say. That was the only thing that kept her ahead of their game.

Screw him. She'd make a life for her and Lucy. Away from the business. Away from this place.

"You must have found out something," Nick said, keeping abreast of her, clearly unfazed that she was preoccupied and ignoring him. "You took long enough."

His impatience made her smile a little. "I told you to go back to the hotel. You should have listened."

He followed her to her car. "I need a ride."

"I'm not going that way."

"How do you know where I'm going?"

She leaned a hip against the car door and stared at him. "Why don't you go back to the hotel bar, get a little smashed, then do whatever attorneys do when they're away from home? I promise not to tell your wife."

One side of his mouth lifted. "You're better than that. I'm sure you know all about me. No wife. No kids." His gaze left her face to wander a casual path down her body before returning to lock with hers. "Just a lot of free time until you find Sands."

"And I just told you how you ought to spend it." She tried to jerk the door open, needing to look anywhere but at the quiet amusement in his dark eyes. This case was going to be what pushed her out of the business for sure. She didn't usually react like this to men, much less a client. But his nearness had her pulse quickening and triggered a nasty little flutter in her belly.

"Come on, Taryn, I'll buy you dinner."

She shrugged, and looked anything but apologetic. "Sorry. I have plans."

"A drink, then?"

Her cell phone rang, and as she slid into her seat to take the call, he rounded the back of the car and got in the passenger side. She waved him to get out and almost gave her mother-in-law an earful before she caught herself.

Instead, she angled away from him. "Yeah, sorry, I'm listening." At Olivia's news, she slumped back. "Why didn't you make it for another night?" The older woman hesitated, and feeling the weight of Nick's stare, Taryn said, "Never mind. I guess I'll see you tomorrow or Wednesday. I'll call."

She hung up before she took her disappointment at not being able to see Lucy tonight out on Olivia. The woman was too old to be raising a ten-year-old. And Taryn should be more grateful. But it seemed Olivia was coming up with more and more excuses to cancel their visits lately.

Maybe she sensed Taryn's edginess and felt her relationship with Lucy was threatened. That was nonsense. Lucy would always be a part of her grandmother's life. The woman had already lost Derek. Probably about the time he turned ten. Taryn wouldn't be so heartless as to keep her granddaughter from her. Not like Taryn's parents had alienated her.

"Got stood up, huh? Tough break. I'll still buy you dinner."

She folded her arms across her chest, leaned back and fixed him with a cold hard stare. "I don't want to eat with you. I don't even like you. You hired me to do a job. I'm trying to do it. When I have something to report, I'll let you know."

He didn't so much as blink. He simply stared back, his eyes intense, probing, trying to break through the barrier she was an expert at maintaining. "What do you feel like? Italian or Chinese?"

Slowly shaking her head and sighing, she pushed

the keys into the ignition. "Italian. I had Chinese last night."

"I didn't think you were the cooking type—"

As soon as she turned the key the radio blasted a Bob Seger song and drowned him out. Good. She pulled the car away from the curb, ignoring the ear-splitting volume.

Travis promptly turned it down. "And here I thought Yanni was more your style."

"Don't try and figure me out. You can't," she said, knowing if he tried another one of the pre-set stations, he'd find out he was partially right.

"I thrive on challenge."

"Good. Try shutting up."

He laughed. "Why do you like playing the tough guy so much? To downplay your looks? You're too smart and competent. Your looks don't get in the way."

She slid him a sidelong glance. He seemed dead serious, and against her will, pride swelled in her chest. And died. This guy had to be playing her. "I haven't found Sands yet."

He shrugged. "What happened upstairs?"

"Nothing much. Maybe I'll get lucky with the mail I swiped. But I didn't get a good-enough look around. He has a nice old neighbor who's convinced Sands will be back, so he keeps a pretty close watch on the place." She sharply exhaled when a rusty white Dodge ran a stop sign and nearly creamed them. As soon as they made it safely through the intersection, she said, "I kind of felt sorry for the old guy."

Silence. She looked over at Travis. He had an odd frown on his face.

"That wasn't my fault," she said. "We didn't have a stop sign. He did."

"I know." His gaze met hers. "Why are you so edgy? Still thinking about your deadbeat date? Give me his address. I'll go beat him up for you."

Not sharing his amusement, she rolled her eyes. "Like I'd need you to do that."

"Oh, yeah, I forgot. You're such a tough guy."

She gritted her teeth. No one teased her like this. And lived. "You can go back to keeping your mouth shut now."

To her amazement, he did. At least for the next ten minutes it took them to get to Ballini's. The place was crowded and noisy and she hoped it made him want to keep dinner short. Unfortunately, although they didn't wait long for a table, it didn't look like they were going to get their meals anytime soon.

More than half the diners already there had nothing but mugs of beer in front of them with an occasional plate of chicken wings or cheese sticks. And here she thought they could easily make it in and out of here within forty-five minutes. She was about to suggest another place when the waitress showed up, her blond hair frizzing, her cheeks flushed and moist.

"Hey, Taryn, you want a beer or are you working?" Sylvia asked, casting a speculative glance at Travis.

"Ginger ale for me." She gestured with a lift of her chin. "Why so busy tonight?"

"Bowling leagues." Sylvia shook her head and blew out a frazzled breath. "At least we'll get rid of them soon. What'll you have?" she asked Travis.

"Beer. Whatever you have on tap." He smiled. "And take your time."

"Maybe we should take a rain check," Taryn said. "You have your hands full."

"Are you kidding?" Sylvia already started walking away. "Free this table up and I'll shoot you. That's the first time I heard 'take your time' in a week."

Taryn laughed. When she returned her attention to Nick, he was staring at her with an odd expression that made the corners of his mouth tilt and his eyes narrow slightly.

She tried to ignore him at first, but his gaze didn't waver. "What?"

He absently shook his head and finally turned away to glance at the next table where the noise was nearing deafening level. A couple with their three hungry kids were squabbling over what kind of pizzas to order.

"You usually don't see many kids in here," she said, hiding her amusement at his sudden interest in their neighbors.

He shrugged. "They have to eat somewhere."

His answer surprised her. And in an odd way, pleased her. Derek had been so impatient with his own daughter. "Do you know what you want?" she asked, pushing the menu toward him.

"You have a recommendation?"

"The spinach pizza."

He grimaced. "You have another one?"

She grinned, and he gave her that strange look again. "The mushroom fettucine alfredo."

"What are you, a vegetarian?"

"Nope. *I'm* having the Italian sausage lasagna."

He gave her a patronizing look, then peered at the menu. The little redheaded boy behind him pushed away from the table and sent his chair slamming into the back of Nick's.

Taryn tensed, waiting for him to explode.

But all he did was glance over his shoulder and say, "Careful, sport."

For the next few minutes, as many times as the trio bumped his chair and squealed in his ear, he continued to study his menu, and remained incredibly tolerant. Much more so than she would have.

He sure did confuse her. She was usually good at figuring people out. But not this guy. Of course, she wasn't generally attracted to her clients. And dammit, as much as she might want to deny it, something about Nick Travis got to her at a very primal level.

Probably a sign she was hanging out with too many lowlifes lately. She saw more muscular bodies at the gym where she worked out. Although admittedly, Nick looked like his body was formed by real work, she thought as she noticed how strong and corded his forearms were. Probably a tennis player. Or mountain climber.

His biceps were developed, too. There was a nicely defined curve that filled out the band of his polo shirt. And did a heck of a job of distracting her.

She quickly raised her gaze to his face. His hair was too short for her liking. Too bad, because he had great hair. Thick, dark, a little wavy. Although not quite a military cut, it was awfully conservative. Which gave him the look of someone her father would have picked out for her.

That should have been enough to make her shudder. Except she had the distinct feeling Nick Travis was anything but her parents' ideal. No matter what his packaging. Or that his manners were impeccable.

Her gaze lingered on the two faded scars near his left eye, the small one by his ear. So faint, they were undoubtedly from childhood. He'd probably been quite a hellion as a kid.

The thought started to make her smile, and then she remembered the not-so-faint scars on his belly. The ones she'd seen when he was almost naked.

And semi-aroused.

Heat seared a path to her very core. She gulped air.

He glanced up, his eyebrows drawing together over eyes that were too dark, too compelling. Too knowing. "You all right?"

No. She needed therapy. "Fine," she said with a little too much bite. "You decided what you want?"

A slow, lazy smile lifted one side of his well-formed mouth and his gaze locked on hers. "Yeah, yesterday."

Chapter Five

Nick watched all emotion drain from Taryn's face. She was so damn good at shuttering her feelings. Talk about ice queen. But in her line of work, that was probably necessary.

So why did he have this asinine urge to penetrate her defenses? Why was he distracting her from her job? He was only screwing himself.

Of course, he needed to get her to open up, too. So far, she hadn't given him squat. Not that he'd expected her to find anything new. Although if she had, he damn well needed to know about it. But at this point, he was more interested in flushing out anyone who was interested in her poking around. So far, no one from the agency had followed her. That surprised him.

He set the menu aside. "So, start from the beginning."

She leaned back, hesitating, a flicker of impatience in her blue eyes the only sign she'd even heard him. "Look, I know it's hard to wait around. But until I find anything of interest, there's really nothing to report. Any conversation is pointless."

He leaned forward. "Then let's consider it fore-play."

Sylvia chose that moment to set down their drinks, her eyebrows arching, her red mouth curving. The ice queen lifted her chin and gave him a cool look, but said nothing until the waitress disappeared.

Then she leaned forward, bringing her face close to his. "This may be a little vacation for you. But this is my livelihood. Don't mess with me."

Her skin was flawless. Almost translucent. Her eyes the purest shade of blue possible. She didn't belong in this place, in this business, in this ugly game of cat and mouse. Guilt suddenly stabbed at Nick for using her.

Cursing to himself, he ruthlessly shoved the emotion aside. There was more at stake here than a bounty hunter. One being paid handsomely to do her job, at that. Besides, she wasn't in any real danger. Unless she did something incredibly stupid. This woman was smart and cautious. That was one of the main reasons he'd hired her.

He leaned even closer. She didn't back up a fraction. "Don't take this personally, Ms. Scott. I'm paying for information. And I do mean to get it."

The threat in his tone clearly didn't faze her. She didn't even blink. Just stared back at him. "If you're unhappy with my work, feel free to take your business elsewhere."

He should do it. There was still time. It wasn't too late to find someone else. Just in case something went wrong. He didn't need another casualty on his conscience. Except he already had involved her. They knew her name. They knew she was trying to resurrect a dead man.

Nick smiled slowly and leaned back, tamping down the adrenaline that was starting to erupt. He was over-reacting. "Can't we compromise?" he asked, picking up his beer and taking an unhurried sip. "You're right. It's tough waiting around. I just want to know what's happening."

She visibly relaxed and mirrored his position by sinking back against her chair. The sudden transformation in her face was startling. Tension seemed to seep from her features. As though she'd just had an epiphany of sorts. And then she gave him a smile that made him want to reconsider his options. Fire her immediately. Keep her as far away from this mess as he could.

He'd seen her rare smile before, but it had never been directed at him. Not like this. Brilliant in its warmth. A ray of sun. A curve of sensuous promise, chasing the darkness from his life.

But only because she knew nothing of him, despite what she thought. Knew nothing of the horrors he'd witnessed, the anguish he'd caused.

"Nick, I—" She let out a quick breath, then started again. "I'm not being fair, and I apologize. My only excuse is that I'm not used to working this closely with a client. I usually work for bondsmen or the courts…" She shrugged. "This togetherness is a little unnerving. What specifically do you want to know?"

Hell, with her abrupt change in attitude, *he* was unnerved. What was going on in that head of hers? "Start from the beginning. I assume you did a computer search and that's how you know his name and social security number haven't surfaced. And that his bank accounts haven't been touched…or that his office…" He paused at the strange look forming on her face. "I did some of that, too. Obviously I had no luck."

She sighed. "Me, neither, but…" She trailed off, and he knew she was deciding if she should withhold something from him.

"What?"

"Nothing, really. It's just that I got a funny vibe at his office. Sands's boss was out, but I talked to a guy named Cross and I got the feeling he was hiding something." Her face creased in a puzzled frown. "In fact, there was something strange about that place. Unfortunately, nothing I can put my finger on. Have you been there?"

He shook his head. "I called once. But no one seemed to have any time for me. That's when I decided to hire you."

"Tomorrow I meet with Harrison Cain, the head honcho. Maybe I'll have some luck there."

"Hopefully. Anything turn up on Sands's background check? Or any recent activity on his bank accounts?"

She pinned him with an amused stare. "I bet you already know the answer to that."

"I didn't find squat on him. You should have. You're the professional."

Her expression turned speculative, then vaguely suspicious. Enough to make him slightly uneasy. "Don't underestimate yourself."

"That, I never do."

She smiled a little. "Know anything about the witness protection program?"

The question came from out of the blue, surprising him, just as she'd meant to do. "Only what I've seen on TV. Why?"

"Oh, I don't know..." She sounded casual enough, but her gaze never strayed from his face. "A guy suddenly disappears like that makes you think..."

"Yeah, I can see why you might wonder. And if it's true, I can assure you, I know nothing about him being in any kind of federal program. I wouldn't underestimate you that much."

Something odd, something he'd almost describe as surprise, maybe even triumph, flared in her eyes before she blinked it away and plucked the straw from her ginger ale. "You ever met Sands?"

"Only on paper." He lifted the frosty mug and took a hearty sip. "Something wrong with the guy?"

"I'm not sure. I mean, he doesn't have a rap sheet, or anything. His tax records are clean, two healthy bank accounts, his credit is impeccable. With all the stuff he's brought into the country, he's never had a single incident with Customs."

"So why the attitude toward him?" He carefully studied her body language.

Something had made her edgy. With one hand, she played with the straw as though it were a cigarette. The other drummed an erratic beat on the Formica tabletop.

"I don't know." Her hand stilled. "He's almost too clean. I'll call one of my friends at HPD tomorrow. With all the trips Sands made in and out of the country, they had to have at least considered that his disappearance had something to do with drugs or smuggling. There's probably nothing to the theory, but I need to check it out."

"Makes sense." He studied her a moment longer. She still hadn't relaxed, although the drumming had subsided. "Something is still eating at you."

She shrugged, stretched the side of her neck. "Not really. I don't like the guy, but most of my bounties are scum buckets. So that doesn't mean anything."

Nick grunted. "You don't like too many people, do you?"

"No, you're in good company."

"Hmm. Scum buckets?"

At his wry tone, she laughed. The pleasant sound was startling. Disarming. Dangerous. "The guy went through women like lemonade on a hot day. Usually flight attendants. I bet most of them never even got a second phone call."

"How the hell did you find out that kind of information?"

Her lips curved in a satisfied smirk. "Maybe one of them did him in."

He frowned, more intrigued than anything else. "What other personal info did you find?"

"He has a penchant for fine wine and usually manages to bring in more bottles from France than his allotment. So obviously he's charming someone in Customs. But when he hadn't been to Europe for a while and had to settle for domestic stuff, he drank a pinot noir from Oregon—Chehalem. Thirty-eight dollars a pop for the '96 Rion Reserve."

She was showing off. Nick stifled his amusement with another sip of beer. "So if he was sneaking in extra bottles of wine, he could have been hiding a lot more."

"Not necessarily. Wine is one thing. You probably get a slap on the wrist for that. Smuggling drugs, diamonds or artwork is something else entirely."

"You think he was involved in things like that?"

She waved a dismissive hand. "No. I'm just making the distinction. Frankly, if he were involved in anything that heavy duty, I figure I would know about it by now.''

''So, basically, just because he's clever enough or charming enough to sneak in a few extra bottles of wine, and he's a bit of a womanizer, you don't like him.''

She gave him a long, hard look. ''The guy was a self-absorbed leech, who made friends only if he could use them. And although it won't affect my job, no, I don't like him. He reminds me of my ex-husband.''

Blinking, she recoiled against her chair, her face draining of color. Clearly, she hadn't meant to reveal that piece of information. ''Ex-husband? I thought he passed away.''

She waved for the waitress. In that few seconds, her mask went into place again, her composure reclaimed with incredible deftness. ''Sands didn't have a single reason to drop out of sight that I can see so far. You'll have to strongly consider the fact that he simply may have had an unfortunate accident.''

''Maybe.'' Right now, he was more interested in her sudden absorption with the menu. And what this new uneasiness meant. Which was insane. He'd waited to play out this game for more than a year. Every strategy planned to the last painstaking detail. Every trail and phone call carefully manipulated. And here he was allowing an asinine fascination with a woman to undermine his final mission.

This foolishness had to stop. Too much was at stake.

Taryn stared blindly at the menu, stewing, yet knowing she wasn't going to get anywhere kicking herself. Except to further throw off her concentration and let more personal information about herself slip.

She tossed the menu aside. So far, no harm had been done. There was no way Travis knew the reason for her reference to Derek as her ex-husband. No one knew that she'd planned on divorcing the bum and running with Lucy the week of his death. Except Derek himself. Or so she had to believe, since all their savings had suddenly vanished the day before Derek was found in that alley, shot with his own gun.

Wanting people to know her business ranked way up there with wanting a root canal, but even if Travis did know…so what? She wasn't going to let the past, or Derek, or any man manipulate her again. Not for love or money. Not for anything.

She lifted her chin, ready to meet her client's annoying and probing eyes. But this time her defenses were in place. No more casual or teasing conversation. No more…

Nick had such a peculiar look on his face, her thoughts scattered like dust in a windstorm. A look of disgust, almost. His gaze started listlessly roaming the room, his interest in her or their conversation no longer existent. What had happened when she wasn't paying attention?

She said nothing and waited for him to resume talking. Sylvia showed up before either of them said another word. In an instant, Nick had pasted on a smile and looked like himself again. He patiently waited for Taryn to order before he asked about the shrimp scampi. And he even made a joke when Sylvia warned him about the amount of garlic the cook used.

Taryn took a sip of her ginger ale and thought about breaking her rule and ordering a beer. Technically she wasn't working at the moment, and this guy had her so wound up it wasn't funny. It was probably just about sex. And not having had any for a while. There was no other explanation she could come up with. Although that was pretty lame, too. She'd never gotten this excited over a sweaty body.

Sylvia left with their orders, and Nick asked, "What time do you go back to the office tomorrow?" His tone was all business, and the smile he'd had for the waitress was gone.

"In the morning," she said, not wanting to get too specific about the time. This chumminess was going to stop after tonight.

"I'll go with you—" he began, and raised a hand to cut off her budding protest. "And wait outside."

"Why?"

"To cover your back."

She stared silently at him for a moment. "And why would I need someone to do that? I thought this was a simple inheritance case?"

"You're the one who brought up drug smuggling. If anything happened to you, I'd feel like crap."

That startled a laugh out of her. "We do need to get you out more. You watch way too much TV."

He didn't even crack a smile, and again she wondered what had set off his bad mood. "Good. What time shall we meet?"

"Oh, no." She shook her head. "That's not the kind of 'out' I had in mind. You're not going with me."

"I won't get in the way. I'll stay outside."

His jaw was set, his eyes harder than granite, and she knew it was hopeless. No matter what she told him, he'd just show up. Unless she threatened to back off the case. But did she really want to kiss off all that money out of stubbornness? Because he really wouldn't be in the way. She just didn't want him around her. And with the way his mood had deteriorated...

"I have an idea. I know how you can help me. Go see if you can get anything more out of Archibald Hanes. The neighbor. Be honest...tell him you're a lawyer and what you want and maybe—"

"No." He cut her off. "I don't want to talk to the old man."

She stiffened at his brusque tone. Did he think she was trying to get rid of him? That was only partly true. "Look, I think I made a tactical error in not explaining what I was really doing there today. This guy really cares about Sands...probably the only person in Houston who does."

Her lame attempt at humor netted a deeper frown from him. "So if Sands had contacted anyone, it would be him."

"Yeah, that, too, but I doubt Hanes has been contacted. I think the guy is still grieving."

"Then it's pointless for me to talk to him."

"Not necessarily. He may know something he doesn't even realize he knows."

His expression grim, Nick stared down at a book of matches he'd picked up off the table. "*You* should talk to him. I may miss a cue and screw something up."

She watched the way he intently focused on the restaurant's logo and wondered what happened to all that enthusiasm to join the hunt. "I haven't abandoned that avenue myself. I left my phone number. The guy is lonely, and I'm counting on him calling me for one reason or another. I just figured it wouldn't hurt for you to see what you could wheedle out of him.''

He raised his gaze to meet hers, his eyes dark and solemn and brooking no argument. ''I can't very well watch your back from across town.''

Taryn sank against the back of her chair and shook her head. She should probably be flattered or grateful or something equally sappy. Not incredulous. Or frustrated. Definitely annoyed.

And truthfully, still a little uneasy.

Because as much as Nick Travis irritated her, raised her defenses, stoked her stubborn streak, his words had ignited a need in her so intense, so astonishing, it made her want to crawl under a table and hide. How long had it been since someone other than Moose had worried about her, or wanted to protect her? Or gave a damn about her?

Except she was too smart to mistake his intentions. This wasn't personal. Nick wasn't offering the tender-loving care or the respect her foolish soul craved. He needed her to get a job done. So he could collect his fee. In the end, it was always about money. Her client's goals surely were no different.

''You're starting to make me nervous,'' she said, teasing, trying to lighten things up. ''Looks like I'm going to have to start looking over my shoulder.''

''Never hurts.''

Silence fogged them for several moments, their gazes dueling until Sylvia set down a basket of bread between them. Five minutes ago, the fresh-baked aroma would have tempted Taryn. But now she couldn't seem to swallow past the dry ache in her throat. A warning that she was missing something. That she was entering the danger zone.

She picked up the bread knife and casually asked, "Want to get anything off your conscience?"

"Such as?"

"Oh, I don't know…" She reached for a slice of the warm bread and concentrated on smearing it with butter, her appetite definitely gone. "Like you're really working for the mob and trying to flush Sands out of the protection program," she said, meeting his eyes at precisely the right moment.

He looked startled at first, and then he laughed. "You accuse me of watching too much TV?" He helped himself to the bread, taking two thick slices, his appetite apparently fine. "Do you think I'd honestly need you if I were working for the—do they still call those people 'the mob'?"

The remark stung. Of course he was probably right. Although she had an impressive recovery rate since working solo, she was a lot pickier about which cases she took, making some clients think it was Derek who'd made Scott Investigations so successful. Business had tapered off to prove it. Yet for some reason, she'd sensed that Nick recognized her competence.

It was that foolish need again, rearing its ugly head, making her long for things she was too wise to wish for. What the hell was the matter with her?

"I don't know," she finally said. "All I'm saying is that it's not too late to get anything off your chest that might make this case easier to solve."

He stopped buttering his bread and stared at her. "If I suddenly admitted I had a less-than-honorable reason for trying to find Sands, you wouldn't necessarily back out? You'd just want to know about it?"

His unexpected question dropped like a boulder, weighing down her shoulders, compressing her chest. She shifted uneasily and was glad to see Sylvia approaching with their meals.

Of course Taryn would drop the case. Even though all that money Travis was offering was a way out for her and Lucy.

Wouldn't she?

Absolutely. Unlike Derek, she had principles.

Except, for a moment, when Travis had posed the question, she honestly hadn't known. She so desperately wanted out of the sewers. So desperately wanted the lies to stop.

All the damn lying. That's what had gotten to her the most. Made her crazy. Made her want to shake Derek senseless. Made her want to disappear forever. Were lies so much easier to tell than the truth? Didn't Derek know she would have accepted just about anything from him if only he'd loved her back?

She took a deep breath and steadied her fidgeting hands when she realized Travis was peering at her with intense curiosity. Good thing she'd grown up and left that foolish notion of blind faith and love behind. Too bad the loss of her own self-respect hadn't been enough. Too bad it had taken her almost losing Lucy to wake up.

But she'd learned her lesson well. And if Travis, or any man, lied to her again and jeopardized Lucy's or her life, she wouldn't think twice about sending him straight to hell.

Chapter Six

Taryn waited until five minutes after ten before she gave up on Nick and took the elevator up to Sands's office. Last night she'd finally agreed to let him wait for her outside this morning, but he hadn't shown up. So much for all that chivalrous bull about wanting to watch her back. He was probably still in bed nursing a hangover. Not that she'd dropped him off at his hotel very late, or that he'd had too much to drink. But she'd had the feeling he was pretty keyed up and not ready to hit the sack when she called it quits last night.

She didn't really give a damn what he'd ended up doing. Her only fear now was that he'd barge in on her when she was talking to Harrison Cain. Of course, even that wouldn't be a big deal. Explaining Nick was easy. She'd told Sands's employer the truth about herself and what she'd been hired to do.

It was also true that she simply didn't want to be around Nick Travis. He resurrected all kinds of unsettling feelings she liked to keep buried deep in the dark part of her memory.

In fairness, it probably wasn't really Nick making her a little nuts. More likely, it was the first anniversary of Derek's death. The grief was over. But the guilt lingered.

As soon as Taryn opened the door, Richard Cross appeared from behind the partition, a phony smile plastered across his pinched face. His lips were thin, as was his nose, and his teeth too big. They annoyed her.

She smiled warmly. "Sorry I'm late."

"No problem. Mr. Cain just arrived himself. Would you like a cup of coffee to take with you to his office?"

She might have been encouraged by this new attitude, but the wariness in the man's eyes warned her not to start breathing easier yet. She didn't drink coffee but politely accepted his offer.

As soon as Cross excused himself, she moved closer to the desks by the window. The tops were neat, mostly clear, except for a couple of sheets of paper sitting by the nearly empty in-box. Her gaze quickly scanned them. Recent faxes, it seemed. Something about a museum opening. Nothing that interested her.

Of course, she wasn't sure what she was looking for. She doubted anything to do with Sands would suddenly pop up. This place just seemed so...

Cross was watching her. Out of her peripheral vision, she saw him standing beside the partition. She moved a little closer to the window and pretended to be fixed on something outside. He still didn't speak for another couple of moments, and then said, "I forgot to ask if you wanted cream and sugar."

She jumped a little, pretending to be startled. "Black is fine." She returned her feigned interest to the window. "Hey, do you know if it's okay to park on the street at this time of day? I'm not going to get a ticket, am I?''

Cross walked over to stand beside her and peered down at the street. His after-shave was sweet and cloying and as irritating as the man himself. ''Where are you?''

Damn. She was parked in the back. She leaned closer to the window and pointed to an obscure spot. ''Over there. Near the intersection.''

''The red Sable? You're okay.''

Taryn's heart thudded. He was right about the make of her car, except there was no way he could see it from here. She glanced down. The rear end of a red car was barely visible. But it looked more like a sports utility vehicle.

She forced a smile, her thoughts racing. ''Good. I can't afford to get another parking ticket.''

''I'd be concerned about more than that.'' He turned to look at her and his face was so close, his black eyes so bleak, her insides rebelled. ''It can be dangerous to park around here.'' His thin lips lifted in a tight smile. ''You're okay for now, but if you come back...'' He paused. ''I wouldn't do it after dark. This isn't the safest area of town, after all.''

Taryn locked her gaze with his. If this slimy little bastard thought he could scare her... ''I think I'll pass on that coffee and go talk to Mr. Cain now. I wouldn't want to stay too long and violate any...uh...parking ordinances.''

Cross gave her a slight bow, his ugly little mouth curling up with satisfaction as he turned away. ''Wise decision. Come with me.''

This was so damn weird. She tossed a final glance at the desk as she turned to follow him. Too neat.

That's what was wrong. The entire place was too orderly. These guys were supposed to be importers, coming and going with odd schedules, no secretaries to keep things in order, yet everything looked so damned perfect.

Anxious to finally get a look behind the partition, she was disappointed when Cross led her down a short hall to the right. It dead-ended at a closed door without a name or title identifying the occupant, but after a brief knock, Cross opened it and stepped aside. It gave her the creeps to have to get so close to him as she sidled by, but she kept her chin up and her shoulders square. If the little creep was expecting her to cower under his thinly veiled threat, he'd better think again. The only thing he'd accomplished was to make her so curious about the place she could spit.

The office was surprisingly large, and at first she didn't see the tall, slender man standing in the corner, gazing out the window until he turned around and gave her a good raking from head to toe. It wasn't a suggestive or hostile look. More curious than anything.

"Mr. Cain?" she said, immediately extending her hand as she approached him.

"Yes," he said absently, "you're that detective."

"Guilty." She shrugged, smiled.

His faded blond hair was graying and his face was weathered from too much sun. His navy blue designer suit was obscenely expensive. In an odd way, he reminded Taryn of her father. Both men were tall and had the same build, the silver in their hair lending more to their distinction than their age. But Mr. Cain had kind blue eyes. And a firm handshake.

"Won't you have a seat?" he said, and released

her hand and gestured to a hunter-green leather chair opposite his desk. He looked past her before he took his own seat. "Is there something you need, Cross?"

She glanced over her shoulder at the other man hovering near the door. He was not pleased at being dismissed like that, judging from the scowl he couldn't quite keep tamped down, and Taryn immediately decided she liked Harrison Cain.

"I just want to remind you that you have several meetings scheduled today. We had to cancel them yesterday because of your doctor's appointment." Cross maintained an even, almost wooden tone. But he was furious. It showed in his eyes. "I trust you don't want to postpone them all again."

Cain didn't answer right away. He leaned way back in his seat and his lips curved in a slow, mocking smile. "I'll let you know. Now, if you wouldn't mind, close the door."

His tone was as civil as Cross's had been, but there was a hint of ruthlessness in his eyes that wasn't there before. A silent message that told the other man to back off. From Taryn? From Sands's investigation? Or something totally unrelated?

In view of Cain's obvious disdain for his assistant, why did he keep the man around? Cross had said Cain was the owner of the agency. This didn't make sense. But was it important to Sands's disappearance? She mentally shook her head. And here she'd thought this was going to be a simple, cut-and-dried case.

At the sound of the door clicking closed, Cain asked, "Well, young lady, what can I do for you?"

She ignored the patronizing way he addressed her. Being underestimated generally served her well. "I don't know how much Mr. Cross has told you, but

I'm trying to find Dylan Sands.'' She went on to give him her spiel, which was the entire truth. As she knew it, anyway.

Cain steepled his fingers, his forehead creasing with thoughtful consideration as he stared off at something over her shoulder. "No one has seen Sands in over a year. What makes you think you can find him?''

"Because I'm good."

A slow, amused smile made the leathery skin around his eyes crinkle. "You know he's probably dead.''

"Maybe. Or else he had a reason to disappear."

"You know of one?"

She leaned back and crossed her legs. Might as well get comfortable. She had a feeling she had a few more rounds to go with Harrison Cain. Maybe it would produce something useful. "I was hoping you did."

Laughing, he pulled out the top drawer of his desk, withdrew a pack of cigarettes and tossed them onto a stack of papers in front of him. "Why?"

Taryn's concentration slipped. For a moment, all she could think about was the pack of Marlboros, calling to her the way a bottle of Ripple seduced a wino. It had been a long ten months since she'd broken the habit. Not because she'd truly wanted to quit, but because Lucy didn't deserve to lose another parent.

She blinked and forced her gaze away from the red-and-white box. Cain was staring at her, measuring her, waiting for her to say something. Taking a deep breath, she pulled herself together. "Making all those trips out of the country and developing such a good rapport with Customs, a man could get tempted to…let's say…bring in something a little extra. I figured that maybe you got wise and threatened him. He decided it was time to cut his losses.'' She shrugged. ''Disappearing with a lot of cash is a whole lot more attractive than going to prison.''

Cain stared at her, transfixed, his lips parting slightly in a look of disbelief. Confusion briefly clouded his face, as though he wasn't sure if this was some kind of joke. And then he blinked and started laughing. So hard, he began to cough.

She let out a huff of air and impatiently waited for him to collect himself. God Almighty. The idea wasn't *that* far-fetched.

He got out a handkerchief and wiped his eyes and nose, and then cleared his throat. ''You do have a vivid imagination. But you're way off the mark.''

''I figured that,'' she said, her tone dry and humorless. Nobody was that good an actor. For whatever reason, Cain found her speculation absurd. ''Although I don't see why that scenario would be so implausible.''

''Not Sands. He was too straight and narrow.''

''That's not the picture I've been getting.''

''I don't know where you've been gathering your information, but I knew that man for ten years and I guarantee you he didn't so much as take a company pencil home.''

Taryn frowned. Okay. Maybe selfish didn't equate to dishonesty. ''So, what's your theory?''

''I honestly think the man is dead. A hiking accident, most likely. He was an avid hiker and a daredevil. Dangerous combination, in my opinion.''

She shook her head. ''That surprises me. He didn't seem the hiking type. More the refined sort.''

He shrugged. "Sands was a chameleon. He could be anything a situation called for. That's why he was so good at his job."

"Importing?"

His eyes evenly met hers, and she swore she saw a flicker of indecision before they went blank. "A lot of the business requires salesmanship. You have to find customers who want the goods. Sands had not only established a solid clientele but one with a good deal of disposable income. As a result, he did quite nicely for himself."

"And for you."

He gave a confirming nod. "Exactly."

She exhaled in frustration. "So as far as you're concerned, he had no reason to drop out of sight."

"None."

She pretended to gaze out the window, but noticed how he fidgeted with the cigarette pack. Which in itself drove her crazy. But she forced herself to focus, because something wasn't quite jiving. His tone and expression were confident, and anyone could easily believe this man knew nothing more than he claimed. But a tension radiated from him, charging the air around them, building a countercurrent to his calm demeanor.

Or maybe it was the nicotine calling.

She wanted a cigarette. Bad.

"Well, that doesn't make sense," she said, forcing herself to relax, her gaze still idly trained out the window. "The guy was probably wrong, or looking for easy money." She deliberately mumbled to herself, but loud enough for him to hear.

"Which guy?"

"What?" she asked, looking up in innocence.

"You just said 'the guy was probably wrong.'" Impatience slipped into his voice. "What are you talking about?"

She waved a dismissive hand. "Some Jamaican fisherman. He claimed he helped a man with Sands's description quietly leave the island. Probably nothing to it. Just hoping for a big reward."

"Probably," he agreed nonchalantly, but his eyes were alert, and she could almost see his mind racing. Finally he picked up the red-and-white box and slowly plucked out a cigarette. So slowly, she wanted to slap it out of his hand. "Care for one?"

She gave him a tight smile and shook her head.

He glanced at his watch as he picked up the silver lighter. "Do you have anything else?"

This interview was obviously over. Her bluff hadn't worked. Not the way she'd hoped, anyway. He wasn't anxious to do any more talking. But still, she'd rattled him a little. She was quite sure of that, and if he lit that damn cigarette in front of her, she was going to do more than rattle him.

"Yeah, there is something else," she said, then at his raised brows, she asked, "Can I talk to some of your other employees?"

"Absolutely," he said without hesitation. "I was going to suggest that myself."

"Great." She eyed the still-unlit cigarette and quickly rose. "Is now okay? If there's anyone around…"

"I think Maynard and Sebastian should both be along at any minute."

"I met Syd Sebastian yesterday. He has a plane to catch in a couple of hours."

"Not anymore," Mr. Cain said, and walked around his desk to open the door. "Anything else for me?"

Taryn hesitated, her thoughts spinning. Cain was being so gracious, she should be glad. And she was. Except he was almost too accommodating. Did Sebastian's canceled flight have anything to do with her? Surely not. Yet, it was sudden, and Cain's tone made her wonder...

She met his eyes. They were too keen, almost anxious. What was she missing? She smiled and extended her hand. "I guess not. Thanks for your time. And all your...help."

"I wish you luck." He clasped her hand. "I always liked the man."

His skin was cool, dry. No sign of nervousness. As she released his hand, she decided to take another shot at him. "Tell you what," she said, lowering her voice. "I have another lead. Someone claims they know where he surfaced." She shrugged, and watched surprise, then alarm flicker in Cain's eyes. "It's probably another wild goose chase, but if I find anything out, I'll let you know."

His face turned so expressionless, she almost thought she'd been fictionalizing his reaction. And then with one small, indifferent lift of his brow, he asked, "Where might that be?"

She hadn't quite expected him to ask her outright. Surely he knew ethically she shouldn't tell him anything. "Boise," she said, the name of the city popping into her head out of the blue. Because that's where Travis was from, of course.

More surprise. More alarm. And then the cool, detached mask again. "Idaho?"

She nodded.

He laughed. "I hope they're paying you well to waste your time." He made a point of looking at his watch again. "But I really have to go. Too many appointments today."

Taking her cue, she started to walk away, but before she made it more than a couple of yards he said, "Ms. Scott, about that fisherman...I wouldn't say—"

She frowned at the abrupt way he cut himself off and was going to ask him what he was about to say when she realized he was looking past her.

Cross.

She saw him out of the corner of her eye, hovering like a pesky mosquito at the end of the hall. Except she was starting to realize he was a whole lot more threatening than a tiny blood-sucking bug. Judging, anyway, by the way Harrison Cain had stiffened.

Instead of finishing his sentence, Cain gestured to Cross and said, "See to it that Ms. Scott gets to speak to both Maynard and Sebastian."

"I'm not sure they'll have time."

"Tell them to make it," Cain said in a voice so stern Taryn couldn't help but openly seek Cross's reaction. "I want everyone to give Ms. Scott their full cooperation."

The younger man's mouth pinched in a tight smile. "Of course."

Before Taryn could toss a glancing thanks at Cain, he'd retreated to his office and closed the door.

The sudden shift in moods and tones made her dizzy. There was clearly an undercurrent she wasn't getting. She sure as hell wished she knew if it had anything to do with Sands.

"Ms. Scott?" Cross was waiting for her. Not even a token smile on his slimy face this time. "Dennis

Maynard is here but not for long, so I'd hurry if I were you.''

As she walked past him out into the reception area, she gave him a smile, mostly because she thought it would irritate him. But then again, she had a feeling her mere existence was enough. It didn't matter. She knew she wasn't going to get anything out of Cross. She just hoped she had better luck with Maynard.

Fat chance.

She eyed the shaggy-haired man wearing too-tight jeans and a pair of thousand-dollar snakeskin cowboy boots. He was half sitting on the corner of the desk closest to the window, his red western shirt so snug it covered his belly like a second skin. Either the guy was clueless, or arrogant enough to not give a damn how silly he looked, and she instinctively knew this was going to be a wasted morning.

Though, it wasn't his appearance but his attitude that convinced her. The moment his chilly green eyes met hers, she knew *clueless* wasn't the right description. His antagonistic gaze burned a hole right through her. Gave her an icy shiver that rocketed straight down her spine. Few people could do that.

''Mr. Maynard?'' She offered him her hand and hoped it came back in one piece. ''I'm Taryn Scott.''

''I know who you are.'' He ignored her hand, so she withdrew it. ''What I can't figure out is why you think that pompous idiot is still alive.''

''Well, don't worry, this shouldn't take long,'' she said in a caustic voice. ''You've already answered two of my questions.''

He lifted a brow in inquiry.

She shrugged. ''You didn't like him and you don't

think he's still alive. And…you're probably actually hoping he isn't.''

A grudging smile lifted the corners of his mouth. His teeth were stained. ''You got that straight. On all three counts.'' He slid off the desk and picked up a mug. ''You want coffee?''

When she shook her head, he looked behind her and held up his mug. ''Make yourself useful, Cross.''

Taryn had almost forgotten about the other man, and glanced over her shoulder in time to hear him utter a foul word, then disappear behind the partition. Without the mug.

Maynard laughed. ''Friggin' spineless idiot. I don't know why they keep him around.''

''They? You mean, Mr. Cain?''

His eyes found hers. Amusement and curiosity made them less cool. But they were still spooky enough to make her want to hurry this interview.

''You got it, babe,'' he said finally. ''So, what is it you want?''

''Reasons why Sands may have wanted to disappear.''

He looked at her a long time, then surprised her by frowning thoughtfully. ''He was a tough guy to figure out. Personally, we didn't get along that good. I didn't know what he did in his spare time and he didn't know nothing about me. We just did our jobs. But I gotta say, the guy probably really did just croak in an accident like Cain thinks.'' He shrugged his beefy shoulders. ''He had it made here. Being the golden boy like he was.''

The door opened, making them both turn.

''Ah, aren't you lucky.'' An oily smile curved

Maynard's mouth as Syd Sebastian walked in. "Here comes his replacement. Cain's new favorite flunky."

Sebastian said nothing, only gave Maynard a look of bored contempt as he dropped his briefcase next to the other desk.

"I bet he has a lot to tell you about Sands," Maynard continued. "I think they might even have been sleeping together."

Sebastian didn't get nearly as ticked as she might have guessed. He turned his back to the other man and smiled at her. However, he wasn't totally immune to the Neanderthal, judging by the tension in his eyes.

"I thought you had a plane to catch," she said, turning her attention to him, pretty much deciding to write off Maynard. She seriously doubted he had anything she wanted. Dennis Maynard clearly orbited a different planet than Sands.

"What?" Maynard cut in. "With a nice little piece of ass like you sniffing around here?"

"Okay." Sebastian took a deep breath and started to turn around, one fist already clenched.

Taryn put a hand on his arm. The last thing she needed was for a brawl to erupt. Not that she thought anyone in this crazy office had a lick of information for her. "I was just leaving," she said. "Want to walk me to the elevator?"

Maynard made a sound of disgust and muttered an obscene word. "I ain't sticking around. Sands ain't coming back. He's dead. And I say good riddance."

No one said another word until the door slammed in his wake. Sebastian unclenched his fist. His chest rose and fell with several deep breaths.

One side of Taryn's mouth lifted. "Just one big happy family."

"Yeah, right." He shook his head.

"Careful, or I'll think one of you bumped off Sands."

Sebastian didn't laugh, didn't even smile, and Taryn got a funny tickle in her chest. His gaze wandered off toward the partition. "Is Cross back there?"

She nodded, feeling a surge of adrenaline. Maybe he had something to tell her, after all.

"Hey, Cross," he yelled. "You got any coffee?"

Hope fizzled. She waited a few seconds, and when Cross didn't respond, she said, "Did you think of anything I might need to know?"

He stared at her for a moment, then shook his head. There was a thoughtful, intelligent look about him, and she hoped that it wasn't interfering with her instincts, but she figured he was telling the truth.

"I'm going to leave you my card," she said, and dug into her purse for one. "Just in case you think of anything. Call me anytime." She paused. This guy seemed to be a genuine friend of Sands, and she'd be scum to inspire any hope. *Damn.* "If it turns out that fisherman really did help Sands leave Jamaica, I'll let you know."

The lie slid so smoothly off her lips it unnerved her. Not a lie. A bluff. This was her job.

And it stunk.

Sebastian's expression became instantly alert. "What fisherman?"

She rubbed her forehead. "Oh, that's right. It was Mr. Cain I told about him. Anyway, it's probably nothing."

"Someone saw Dylan?" His gaze darted toward

the hall, then the partition. Disbelief thicker than Vermont syrup coated his lowered voice. "Recently?"

Why did he find that so incredible? Did he know something about Sands's death? "Almost a year ago."

He blinked and stared at the wall, until a slight smile began to curve his lips. "Son of—" He shook his head, but this time, not in disbelief. An odd gleam entered his eyes. He looked pleased. Very pleased.

"Do you remember something?" she asked quietly, trying to tamp down her own excitement.

His gaze settled on her, a distant look in his eyes, as though he'd forgotten she was there. Immediately all emotion left his face, and an expressionless mask fell into place. "Sorry. Nothing."

Taryn reared her head back. "You could've fooled me."

He gave her a sharp look before resuming a passive expression. "He was my friend. If he did take a powder, then good for him. He had to have his reasons. But it sure isn't up to me, or you, to drag him back to hell."

She straightened. *Hell? Here?*

"I doubt we have anything else to discuss." He put out his hand. "Maybe I can still catch my plane, after all."

So he had stuck around for her. Under Cain's instructions?

She thought about asking him a few more questions, but the sudden implacable look in his eyes told her she'd be wasting her time. She accepted his handshake instead.

"If I find anything out, you want me to let you know?"

He released her hand, then hesitated. Behind his unreadable eyes, a war was waging. Was he trying not to look too anxious? Was he concerned about his friend? "Sure. I guess."

He picked up his briefcase and they walked out together. Taryn briefly thought about sticking around, but the idea of dealing with Cross again turned her stomach. She would've done it, anyway, if she believed it would get her anywhere, but at this point, she knew better.

That was the unfortunate thing about investigative work. You had to explore every little detail, no matter how obscure or inconsequential it seemed. Sometimes it paid off. Mostly the process sucked.

Today she may not have found out anything concrete, but she sure as hell was starting to believe Sands could be alive. And she'd bet everyone in his office knew a lot more than they were willing to tell.

They stopped at the elevator and Taryn punched the down button.

Beside her, Sebastian grunted. "Damn, I forgot something. You go ahead. I have to run back to the office."

She didn't believe him. He seemed distracted enough, but she had the feeling his preoccupation had to do with Sands. So did this sudden detour. Not that she could do anything about it. She smiled. "Have a safe trip."

"Yeah, thanks."

The elevator doors opened, and she stepped inside and watched him hurry back to the office. She'd give just about anything to be a fly on the wall in there. Maybe she ought to bug the place. If she could even get her fanny back in there without Cross getting in her face.

It was another hot, humid day and she was suddenly glad to be out in it. But by the time she got to her car, some of her pleasure faded. The itch between her shoulder blades meant one thing. Someone was watching her. If it was Travis again, she was going to wring his neck.

In case it wasn't, she slid a furtive look around as she climbed into her car.

Nothing. Not even Travis.

She rubbed the back of her neck and left the door open while she started the car and got the air conditioner going. A glance in the rearview mirror produced nothing unusual, but the shaky feeling didn't go away.

Cross hadn't answered when Sebastian had called out to him. Had he somehow slipped out to wait for her? Hell, he already knew what kind of car she drove. Her business card told him where her office was. He wouldn't need to follow her.

Unless he thought she was close to finding Sands.

She glanced again in the rearview mirror, then the side mirror, and finally pulled out into the street. If anyone was following her, he was going to be sorely disappointed to find that she was only going back to her hole-in-the wall office.

Taking the most direct route, she got there in twenty minutes, then parked in her usual spot. Outside of the deli where she often picked up a sandwich for lunch, she hesitated. Adrenaline had started pumping in earnest about five minutes ago, squelching her appetite. If someone was following her, it was a good sign, and she almost hoped he was.

She decided not to break routine and took a step toward the deli door. That's when she saw him. A few feet behind her.

Her heart plummeted. "Dammit, Travis. I told you—"

Cutting her off, he pulled her roughly into his arms, grabbed a handful of hair, tipping her head back, and captured her mouth with his.

Chapter Seven

Taryn gasped, but only managed to lose more of the precious air she needed. She tried to raise her hands to push him away, but he held her so tightly, she couldn't get any leverage. When she tried to back up, his fingers twisted deeper into her hair. His mouth pressed harder.

The hot afternoon sun singed the air around them and pelted them with so much heat, Taryn was getting slightly dizzy. Her fists relaxed a little, her fingers uncurling until she clutched at Nick's shirt.

The movement encouraged him. He pulled her head back further, until his tongue slipped between her surprised lips. He swept her mouth, leaving behind the faint taste of mint and masculinity.

What the hell was he doing? She had to tell him to stop. They were on a sidewalk, for God's sake, in front of...

She breathed in his musky scent, savoring the way it seemed to seep into her skin and fill all those empty pores of longing. When his tongue dove deeper, she didn't push him away. She clung to him, not with her hands, but with her deep-seated need to be held. Be wanted.

To her shame, Nick shifted away first. His gaze briefly swept her face, then lingered on her lips. "Check out the white van behind me," he said softly.

White van? She blinked, confusion then indignation slicing through the sensual web he'd woven. The kiss had been for show. Why it had been necessary, she didn't know yet. Only that it meant nothing personal.

For a moment, she thought about kneeing him. Not that her boneless legs were much good to her right now. Instead she breathed deeply, trying to regain her wits, but she could still smell him, hot and tempting, and the sensation made her weak again.

"You okay?" he asked, pulling her closer, his eyes darkening, his brows drawing together, as if in concern.

His face was too close, his gaze probing, too knowing. She gave him a curt nod and averted her eyes, not wanting him to see any longing in them.

She swallowed hard, then scanned the block. Several car lengths away was the van. Late-model. Tinted windows. No passenger that she could see. Just the driver. But between the sun's glare and the heavy tinting, she couldn't be sure. Like the rest of her traitorous body, her vision still wasn't back to normal yet, either.

"See it?"

"Yeah. But I don't think it followed me." She started to move away. He ran his hand down her back until it rested at the curve of her rear, and pulled her in closer still.

She sucked in a breath when his face moved toward hers again. But he only placed a light kiss at the corner of her mouth. "A little overkill, don't you think?" she asked, and silently cursed at her breathlessness.

"Let whoever's in the van think we're too busy to notice him. That you're off the clock."

She snorted. "He didn't follow me."

Using a knuckle, he lifted her chin. "Humor me."

His eyes had darkened and were focused intently on her, and the hunger she saw there made her pray that whoever was in the van hadn't followed her, because if they had, she was in deep trouble. Her instincts had gone haywire. The insane desire to respond to Nick was so totally unlike her that the realization alone was staggering. Sobering.

Fortunately, she knew he was wrong. No one had followed her. She'd been careful about checking. Unless... Her troubled gaze strayed back to the van. Could someone be following Nick?

"Let's duck in here for a while and get a table by the window." He gestured with a slight tilt of his head to the bar next to her office. "We can keep an eye on him. If he leaves, we'll know you're in the clear."

"Maybe he's following you," she said, watching for his reaction.

"Me? Why?" He looked mildly surprised, then his gaze lowered to her mouth and his face started moving toward hers again.

She turned away and caught the disapproving frown of an older woman hurrying her two small children past them. "Knock it off, Travis. I think you've distracted the guy enough. Assuming he is watching us."

Or was Nick trying to distract her?

The uneasy thought seeded and blossomed like an

uncontrollable weed, squeezing everything out but doubt and suspicion, and she shoved him away.

He abruptly stepped back, eyeing her with guarded interest.

"You coming?" After another furtive look at the van, she headed for the bar.

Nick followed close and arrived at the waist-high table nearest the window in time to pull out a bar stool.

Unsmiling, she dropped her purse on it, deciding to stand.

Nick used his boot to nudge the other stool out of the way and stood beside her. Close enough that his shoulder rubbed hers. "You look like you're ready to put a fist through a wall. You recognize the driver?"

"The guy isn't following me." She turned to look him in the eyes. "He must be following you. Why?"

He shrugged, keeping his unreadable gaze level with hers. "No way. What would anyone want with me?"

"I don't know. Enlighten me."

A lazy, unconcerned smile curved one side of his mouth and he briefly transferred his attention out the window toward the van. "I don't have a clue. Most people run the other way when they see a lawyer coming."

"Where were you this morning?"

He cringed. "I overslept." He looked abashed enough that she wanted to believe him. "How did your meeting go?"

She ignored his question and carefully watched his face for clues. "What made you think the van was following me?"

"I got to Sands's office just about the time you

were pulling out of your parking space and I had the cab driver follow you. I only noticed the van because I'd been thinking of getting one just like it a few months ago. After a few miles, I realized he seemed to be dogging you.''

Taryn leaned back and considered his explanation. He looked earnest enough, but Nick interested in a nondescript family-type van? She didn't think so. Except the genuine concern in his gaze as it kept returning to the window wasn't for show. It was real. If Nick was telling the truth, it meant she'd missed being tailed. By both him and the van.

Damn Nick Travis. She was acting like a stinking rookie, thanks to him. She unclenched her teeth. ''Did you get a look at the driver?''

He shook his head. ''He was always slightly ahead of the cab. And the windows are heavily tinted.''

''I took a busy route. It could be a coincidence.''

''Could be.'' He slipped an arm around her shoulders, and she glared at him, but he was looking past her out the window. ''I guess we'll find out soon.''

She seriously thought about jabbing him between the ribs. She knew how to aim for the right spot that would put him out of commission until she finished the case.

He finally met her glare and amusement awakened in his dark eyes. ''Don't make me kiss you again,'' he warned.

She shifted her elbow just enough to let him know she was capable of inflicting pain. ''You do, and you'll be looking for another investigator.''

He grunted slightly at the pressure, then smiled. ''Keep it up, Taryn, and I'll think you like my advances.''

"In your dreams, Travis." She straightened when she thought she saw the door of the van open. But it was a trick of the sun's glare.

"Honey, you don't know the half of it." He followed her gaze, but he was careful not to be too obvious. He smiled at a passing waitress, then pretended to read a tent card on the table advertising a drink special. All the while his attention remained discreetly in tune with the activity beyond the window. He was good at surveillance. Too good.

Taryn shifted away from him and tossed her hair to shake it loose when it clung to his arm. "I think we did the loving couple bit long enough. Not that I ever saw the point to it."

He turned toward her with a growing smile, but it died when his gaze touched her hair. And then he slowly lifted a hand and rubbed a few strands between his thumb and finger.

At the blatant desire smoldering in his eyes, a thrill shot through her. Made her heart pound in anticipation.

Heat. Slow, churning waves of heat rolled over her. Until it became panic, like an undertow, sucking her under, filling her lungs. She fixed her attention on the van and ignored Nick for all she was worth.

"You two want anything besides each other?"

They both turned. The young, half-dressed waitress cracked her gum and grinned.

"Two ginger ales," Nick said, unsmiling, then turned back to studying the van. His jaw was tense except for the small tic he obviously couldn't control.

Not sure her voice was working and glad she didn't have to order, Taryn continued to concentrate on the van. She'd barely let it out of her sight for more than a few seconds, and still no one had left or entered the vehicle. Made her wonder if Nick was right about it.

When the young woman was well out of earshot, he asked, "What happened at Sands's office?"

"Strange place." She shook her head. "Strange people."

"Who did you talk to?"

At his take-charge tone, Taryn's initial reaction was to clam up. But she knew how he could be like a dog with a bone. He wasn't going to let go. And truthfully, there was no reason for her not to share the information. "Harrison Cain, the owner. Nice guy, cooperative, seems to have a fondness for Sands, but I'm pretty sure he's holding back something."

"Who else?" Impatience underscored his tone as his gaze stayed trained outside.

Funny, why hadn't he asked more about Cain? And why she thought he might be holding something back? "Dennis Maynard. What a loose cannon he is." She watched Nick's jaw tighten. The pulse at his neck beat erratically. "You know him?"

"I know that he works in Sands's office."

"That's all?"

He looked away from the van long enough to give her a measuring glance. "Should I know more?"

"You reacted to his name."

"I was reacting to the van door opening."

Her gaze shot to the van.

"But I was wrong," he said. "A reflection made it look like it was opening. So tell me about this Maynard."

She gritted her teeth. He was smooth, all right. Enough to make her second-guess herself. "A real sweetheart. The guy doesn't like Sands so he wasn't any help. Except..."

At her pause, he slid her a mildly questioning look. She'd hoped for more of a reaction.

"Except that he doesn't fit the image of the company man."

His attention returned to his vigil. "Am I supposed to guess the punch line?"

She ignored his sarcasm. "Cain said part of the job is salesmanship, and he described Sands as being a chameleon, which made him perfect for his job. As far as I know, Sands and Maynard both did the same thing. But Maynard would have to be more than a chameleon to have any customers. I can't think of anyone in their right mind who would trust this buffoon to buy them a stick of gum, much less valuable imports."

"Your point is?"

She shook her head. "Something isn't right. Cain wears thousand-dollar suits and his office is a dump."

"Just because the guy has a clothes fetish doesn't make him a suspect."

The amusement in his voice grated on her nerves. Then again, maybe his light take was a good sign he had no hidden agenda. "Of course, there's also Richard Cross," she said, and at Nick's clear indifference, she added, "And the fact that he knows what kind of car I drive."

That got his attention. He turned to frown at her, and she automatically took over surveillance of the van. "How do you know?" His demand was curt, his body suddenly tense.

"He slipped, but he called it right down to the color." She took a quick breath and shook her head.

"I don't know. Maybe he didn't slip. I think it was a warning."

Nick's narrowed gaze slowly returned toward the street. Tension radiated from him in spite of the fact that he was trying hard to look relaxed. "Could be Cross in the van, then."

"Could be." She stared at him for a moment. Dammit, did he know something? "Not too late to come clean, Travis."

His mouth lifted slightly. "Sorry to disappoint you."

Her eyes stayed fixed on his well-shaped lips. She recalled how they felt pressed to hers, how their searing imprint still lingered. What was it about this particular man that had her so wound up? She raised her gaze to find him watching her.

She cleared her throat just as the waitress showed up with their drinks. But even after the woman left, Nick's gaze hadn't wavered. If anything, it had intensified, making his eyes even darker, his desire clear.

"If anyone is following me," she said, annoyed at the breathlessness she heard, "which I am yet to be convinced of, my money would be on Cross. After Syd Sebastian arrived, I didn't see Cross again. He didn't answer when Syd called out for coffee, either. Could be he slipped out a back door and was waiting for me down the street."

She'd been watching the van again, but when he didn't respond, she looked over at him. A thoughtful frown drew his dark brows together.

"You didn't tell me you talked to Syd." There was an odd, unidentifiable note in his voice. But his reference to Sebastian caught her more immediate attention. "What did he have to say?"

"Obviously you know him."

"What?"

"You called him Syd."

He shrugged and sent her a brief look that said she must be crazy. "Just taking your cue."

There it was again. That odd tone of voice. She briefly replayed the last few minutes of their conversation in her head.

"Tell me about him," he said, breaking into her thoughts before she could make head or tail of them.

"He was cooperative. Seemed to have been on good terms with Sands. But I think he's holding something back, same as Cain."

She blinked, finally realizing that she'd referred to Sebastian by his first name while using everyone else's last. There was no significance to it, of course. For a moment, she'd figured she'd caught Travis in a lie, but he'd merely been taunting her.

"What is it you think *Syd* is holding back?" Nick asked, with an amused lift of one brow, and she wanted to smack him.

"I told him I'd found a Jamaican fisherman who'd helped Sands off the island," she said, and he stiffened, his watchful eyes drawing back to her face. "That seemed to throw him off balance. And then he looked as though he remembered something, but he wouldn't talk."

"Where were Cross and Maynard?" He looked serious again.

"Maynard had already left, but Cross could have heard me. Why?"

He picked up his ginger ale for the first time and took a long, slow sip as he turned his attention back toward the van. As if he were stalling. "Just trying to piece the puzzle together," he finally said. "Where did you hear this fisherman story?"

"I didn't. Just doing a little fishing myself."

"So, you made it up."

Taryn bristled at his censuring tone. It wasn't as if she was lying. It was her job to bait people.

"Anything else I should know?" He was back to indifference.

She grunted. "Don't push it, Travis. I don't owe you a blow-by-blow report. What I just gave you was pure charity."

He smiled at that but didn't look at her. "You don't give an inch, do you?"

"Hell, I just gave you a mile." She squinted at a man approaching the van, but he kept walking past it. If it was Cross tailing her, he already knew where her office was. He was going to be ticked and disappointed. Which made her hope it was him. "This is a waste of time. I should be at my computer."

"You don't think it's strange that someone pulls into a parking space but never gets out?"

"They could be picking someone up."

"Humor me. Let's wait another fifteen minutes."

"Ten."

His mouth curved again, and she bit back a curse when it made her stomach flutter. "Another question," he said.

She sighed with disgust. "Yeah?"

"Have you started dating since your husband's death?"

Leaning heavily on the table, she let out a sound of exasperation. "None of your damn business."

"True." He looked over at her, letting his gaze

drift down the front of her blouse where she'd undone two buttons in deference to the heat. Had he lingered three more seconds, it would have been considered insolent. Instead, his look sparked a longing so penetrating it gave her a shiver.

Made her nipples tighten. Her soul ache.

She sucked in a breath and let it out slowly.

"Give up on the van?" she asked when he wouldn't quit watching her face.

"I've got it covered." He frowned a little. "I made you nervous."

She snorted. "I'm impatient and unconvinced we're doing anything useful. Not nervous." She started digging in her bag for her cell phone. "I'm calling my answering service, and then I'm leaving."

"I bet Syd made a play for you."

She stopped and stared. "You know this guy, don't you?"

He shook his head. "Just a guess."

A laugh threatened. Here she thought he was preoccupied with some hidden agenda, and he was speculating about her love life. He probably wanted her to ask him how he'd come up with that theory about Syd, but she wasn't going to. The conversation would only end up getting personal again. She continued rooting until she located her phone.

"Too bad we didn't meet under different circumstance," he said. "I would really have liked getting to know you."

Taryn was ready with a flip remark, but the look of genuine regret on his face stopped her cold. And then it was gone and he was looking out the window again.

She took a quick sip of ginger ale and started dialing her answering service. For the life of her she couldn't come up with a suitable reply. She didn't feel like being flippant anymore. In fact, she had the craziest notion to ask him why they couldn't get to know each other.

Which was beyond insane. She was through with men. Especially ones who liked to varnish the truth. And though Nick seemed to have all the answers, she still wasn't sure he was telling her everything.

The answering service had only three messages. The first two were from bail bondsmen with small recovery jobs for her. She quickly scribbled down the information to call later. But she had a feeling this case was going to occupy the rest of her week. Cut and dried, she'd thought. Right.

The last message made her pulse quicken. It was from Archibald Hanes. He'd decided to let her into Sands's apartment.

"Bingo," she said as she hung up. "The neighbor called."

Nick's brows drew together. "I thought you said he was just a lonely old man who probably didn't know anything. Sounds like a waste of time."

She frowned at the sharpness in his voice. "I still don't think he knows anything. I'd just rather enter the apartment without breaking in."

"He'll watch you like a hawk. How do you expect to get anything out of there?"

"Let me worry about that. If I only get an address book, I'll be pretty damn happy."

"I already gave you a list of contacts."

"Pardon me, but I thought you were paying me to be thorough. Besides, you missed at least one key person."

He stiffened. It wasn't her imagination. She saw it in the rigid set of his shoulders, the tightness around his mouth. Was this about his ego? Or was she getting close to something she wasn't supposed to?

"Who?" he asked slowly.

"Priscilla Racine. A flight attendant. Sands went out with her, from what I gather, but I don't know any more. I found her name through his traffic history. He had a minor accident with her in his car one evening some time ago."

Surprise, then something...admiration, maybe... glinted in his eyes. "I knew about her," he said, losing all expression. "In fact, I spoke with her. She's a dead end. Don't waste your time."

"Maybe." Watching him closely, she shrugged. "I'll let you know after I talk to her."

He scrubbed at his eyes and exhaled a long, weary sigh. "I'd rather you didn't."

"Why not?"

"Because I know for certain she won't be of any help and I'm in a bit of a time crunch."

"You didn't say anything about a deadline."

"You thought the case would be wrapped up fairly quickly," he reminded her.

She winced. Hell, it had been only two days since she'd started poking around. But unfortunately, she was getting nowhere. "What? You get a bonus if you find him by a certain date?"

If he was faking the guilty chagrin clouding his face, he was good. "I'll split it with you."

Sighing, Taryn focused on her cell phone. Always about money. She dialed the number Hanes had left, wondering what was really eating at Nick. There had to be something more to him not wanting her to go back to Sands's apartment or meeting with Priscilla Racine.

He respected her competency. That's one of the things she did like about him. So she was surprised he questioned what she deemed a useful lead. Maybe it was a simple matter of him having other plans for her this afternoon. Like going back to his hotel room. Well, he could think again.

He watched her punch in the last number, his irritation at her stubbornness clearly growing.

She pushed the send button.

His jaw tightened as he turned away from her to stare out the window again. Sulking wasn't going to change her mind. But if it shut him up, that was okay.

Mr. Hanes answered quickly and they agreed to meet at his apartment in half an hour. Nick shot her several odd looks during the course of the short conversation, and she had to admit, her curiosity was piqued. He seemed tense, edgy, although he hid it fairly well. But the tic at his jaw gave him away every time. He was convinced the van had followed her. Maybe that was unnerving him. He wasn't used to this kind of work.

"What do we do about the van?" he asked.

She thought for a minute. Maybe she could get rid of Nick in case she *was* being followed. "We each go our separate ways. If someone is following he'll have to choose one of us."

"I don't like it."

She picked up her purse. "Too bad."

He put a hand on her arm and lightly stroked her skin with his thumb. "I think we should stick together."

She stared at his hand for a moment, how his fingers wrapped around her slender forearm. Protective, almost. When she raised her gaze to meet his, she found a flicker of concern before he shut out all emotion.

"I doubt they're following you," she said.

"I know."

He really was worried about her. Which was laughable, considering the scum she'd tracked and brought in. But Nick didn't know that.

She smiled gently, wanting to allay his fears. "I'll be fine." She withdrew her arm from beneath his hand, but surprised herself by giving his palm a squeeze. Only a drop of guilt plagued her for wanting to get rid of him. Her reason wasn't strictly personal. His nearness was a danger to her. And if someone was following her, she might be a danger to Nick.

He leaned back and ran a frustrated hand through his hair. She could tell by the resigned slump of his shoulders he knew she wouldn't give in. "This stinks." He shook his head. "Where do we meet?"

"I'll call you at your hotel." She slid off the stool, anxious to go before he could argue.

"I can't sit around and wait."

She didn't want him staying here. If the van did pull out after her, he was likely to run to the rescue and get himself hurt. Or killed.

"Come on, Nick." She put out her hand. "Walk me out, then grab a cab."

His startled gaze fastened on her outstretched palm, then went to her face. "You're not softening up on me, are you?"

"As squishy as a marshmallow."

His eyes narrowed in suspicion, but he took her hand and got up, at the same time laying money on the table. "You'll call me as soon as you leave Sands's apartment."

"Yes," she said, trying not to think about his touch, how good it felt. How long it had been since...

Of course she'd be crazy to attach any emotion to the contrived gesture. Especially since they each had their own private agenda. As soon as they got outside, she let go.

Nick apparently wasn't so anxious to break contact. He lifted his hand and, holding her chin, placed a brief kiss on her lips. "For luck."

She exhaled, stepped back. "I'll call. Now, go."

He didn't say anything, just put on his sunglasses and moved back, slipping his hands into his pockets. His attention was directed toward the van, although he did a good job of hiding it. She continued to watch it from a reflection in the laundromat's window across the street.

Not until she climbed into her car did he saunter away in the opposite direction. She turned the key but waited another minute, pretending to refresh her lipstick.

The van didn't move.

She pulled away from the curb and a large truck temporarily blocked her view. When she could see again, the van was gone.

She checked her rearview mirror, the side mirror. When she turned around she thought she got a glimpse of it heading the other way. The same way Nick was headed.

In the middle of the intersection, she screeched into a U-turn.

Chapter Eight

After backtracking a mile toward downtown, Taryn cruised the side streets, and still saw no sign of the van. Or Nick. It was as though they'd both vanished into thin air.

It was entirely possible Nick had flagged a cab right away, though not likely. Not in Houston.

She tried calling him at the hotel, but with no luck. Of course, he probably wouldn't have made it there yet. Taking several deep breaths, she steered the car toward Sands's apartment. And picked up the cell phone again.

It was stupid to be this worried about Nick. The van's leaving was probably a coincidence. Or else it would have followed her. She checked her rearview mirror again as she'd done regularly. A late-model black Lincoln was a ways back.

On the other hand, if the van had followed Nick, she should be ticked off, not worried about him. It meant he'd been hiding something, just as she'd suspected.

She slammed the steering wheel with the heel of her hand. What happened to her nerves of steel? Her insides were jumping around like something was on fire. Acting like a rookie again. Just like she had the first few times Derek had taken her with him to track bail jumpers. Before she'd started thrilling to the chase.

But the time had come when she looked forward to climbing behind Derek on his bike, or felt the excitement of jump-starting their second-hand truck because they were so sure they'd pick up a skip that day.

The good times were often hard to remember, they were buried under so many of the toxins that poisoned their marriage. Derek had been like a drug to her. She couldn't get enough of the danger, the freedom from societal mandates, the wildness he represented and that her parents despised.

Her laugh was rueful as she pulled the car into a space a block from Sands's apartment. No, finishing school hadn't warned her about someone like Derek. Not that it would have done any good if she had been forewarned. Addiction obeyed no rules.

She tried calling the hotel one last time even though she'd already left a message for Nick to call her cell phone. When she didn't get an answer, she impulsively punched in her mother-in-law's number, feeling an overwhelming need to talk to Lucy, the only good thing to come out of their marriage. To have her, Taryn would have done it all over again.

The line was busy. And knowing Olivia, she'd be talking to her friends for hours. Disappointment weighed heavily as Taryn disconnected the call, then crossed the street. She didn't know why she suddenly needed the reassurance of her daughter's voice. Maybe a reminder that this case was worth it. That it could buy their freedom. That she wouldn't have to look over her shoulder for the rest of her life.

Mr. Hanes opened the door before she took her hand off the doorbell. His faded gray eyes were bright and eager, and she wondered if he ever had company now that Sands was gone.

"Come in." He gestured expansively with one hand while resting on his cane with the other. "I just made tea."

She gave him a polite smile. "I really don't have time for tea. And I don't want to disturb you. Maybe you could just let me into Dylan's place?"

His shoulders sagged and disappointment etched fine lines across his forehead. "Of course. You young people are so busy these days." He gave her a weak smile and grabbed a key ring and a large watering can from somewhere behind the door. "I've saved my chores for when you collect your things."

She smiled and stepped aside so that he could come out of his apartment. She hadn't really expected to have the run of Sands's place. At least Hanes would be preoccupied and not breathing down her neck.

He chatted all the way down the hall to Sands's door about nothing in particular, and she paid little attention until he stopped abruptly. He had just unlocked the door and pushed it open, but now stood frowning at something behind her. She turned around and saw Nick coming toward them.

Her heart did a funny little skip at the sight of him. Relief and elation tangled in her chest. The swift onslaught of gratitude throwing her off balance, she took a quick breath.

Then she glared at him. She was glad he was okay, but if Hanes didn't let her in now, she was going to...

Mr. Hanes blinked, then squinted. Using his cane for support, he leaned forward. He seemed confused. "Can I help you, young man?" he called out, as he pulled the door shut again and stared warily at Nick.

She gave Nick the eye, willing him to keep walking, pretend he was on the wrong floor. Anything but...

"I'm with her." Nick stopped and smiled.

Hanes's suspicious gaze flicked to Taryn, then back to Nick. His expression grew even more cautious. "Is this your new beau?" he asked. "Couldn't wait for Dylan to come home?"

"Oh, no—" Her denial died as Mr. Hanes lumbered past her to stand face-to-face with Nick.

"You're Dylan's brother, aren't you?" the old man asked, peering closely at Nick.

Nick shook his head. "Actually, I'm Taryn's brother."

She didn't dispute him. His quick thinking would probably appease Hanes. But what mostly kept her silent was Hanes mistaking Nick for Sands's brother. Wouldn't he know Sands didn't have a brother? Or did he know something they didn't?

Hanes sighed. "Pardon these worn out old eyes," he said, but still seemed confused. He gave Nick another thorough looking over, and shook his head. "You resemble my friend, Dylan. But of course he's got lighter hair and eyes. Has a more prominent snout, too."

Nick's mouth curved in a tolerant smile. He was probably thinking the same thing she was. Hanes's grief was playing tricks on him. Taryn had seen two different photos of Sands. Nick looked nothing like him. They were about the same height and build. That's all. But if there *was* a brother, she sure wanted to know about him.

Hanes finally turned away to unlock the door again. "Since you're her brother, I guess it's all right to let you in, too."

"Good. I have an ulterior motive for coming with Taryn," Nick said, and ignored the warning look she slid him. "I heard you had an interesting orchid collection."

Pushing open the door, Hanes beamed at him. "Are you an enthusiast?"

"No, just an admirer. There's no green thumb on my hand, I'm afraid."

Hanes laughed with sheer delight, and even Taryn had to smile at the charm Nick was oozing. She hoped they were on the same wavelength. If he kept Hanes busy showing off his orchids, it would give her a chance to snoop.

They entered the apartment, and Hanes went directly to a china pot loaded with fragile white blooms. Taryn wanted to ask more about the possibility of a brother, but she figured this was a good time to slip away unnoticed.

"Take a look at this," Hanes said with pride in his voice. "Everyone from my correspondence garden club said I would never be able to grow a Cybidiun in Houston." He shook his head sadly. "Patience. Nobody has patience anymore. And ingenuity. You must see my greenhouse. It's out on my terrace." He paused, and frowned at a petal. "In fact, Zelda here is going to have to go home. Not enough humidity in here for a prolonged visit."

"I'll carry her if you like." Nick didn't even give Taryn a fleeting glance as she disappeared into the bedroom before Hanes remembered she was there. "That way I can see your greenhouse at the same time."

Taryn listened by the door to see if Hanes missed her, impressed and a little surprised by the gentle way Nick handled the elderly man. Not a trace of impatience tainted his voice as he asked intelligent-sounding questions about the orchids and listened to long, boring answers.

She thought briefly about dinner last night and his tolerant reaction to the squealing children at the next table. They had gotten on her nerves, but he'd even smiled at the little tyrants as they left the restaurant.

He was going to be a terrific father some day, she thought, the sudden idea unnerving her. Or maybe it was the unexpected wistfulness seeping in that was unsettling. Or maybe simply having turned thirty-one last week was getting to her.

Her attention snapped back to the men, the idea that it had wandered annoying her. She had to focus, get as much information as she could while Hanes was distracted. The answering machine would be her first stop after they left. That Sands would have a message after all this time interested her. Probably just some damn telemarketer. Or maybe she'd get lucky.

"What can I help carry back to your place?" Nick asked, his voice loud enough for her to get the message.

"These two would be of great help, if you'd be so kind."

Seconds after she heard Hanes's voice, his cane

tapped a path across the marble foyer. She checked her watch and gave herself five minutes to gather as many things as she could.

The door opened and she started to relax, letting the strap of her bag slide off her shoulder.

"Ah, Ms. Scott?"

At the sound of Hanes's voice she froze. "Yes?" Smiling, she stepped into the bedroom doorway.

"We'll only be a moment." Hanes returned the smile. "Shall I put on some tea?"

She hesitated. What she wanted to do was grab what she could and get out, but she sensed that her freedom to accomplish that weighed heavily on her answer. Looking briefly at Nick, she shrugged. "We can stay for at least one cup."

"Splendid." Hanes started out the door, stopped and asked, "You don't mind being left on your own, do you?"

Taryn shook her head, her gaze drawn to Nick's face. He was unhappy about something. Probably having to stay for tea. Tough. "Do you want me to come to your apartment when I'm done, or shall I wait here for you?"

"Why don't you come around? My leg has been acting up today."

Perfect. She smiled again as they left the apartment, Hanes chatting away, Nick stone-faced. As soon as she figured they were far enough down the hall, she went for the answering machine and pressed the play button.

"Hi, it's Priscilla. I'm at home. Call me." That was the only message. Not what Taryn was hoping for. And then the machine gave the date and time the message was left. Five months ago.

She frowned. Sands had already been missing for over seven months by then. This woman sounded like she'd talked to him a few days ago. Priscilla Racine just moved up to the top of the list.

After making sure there were no old messages, Taryn rooted through some mail, the drawers to both the desk and the bedroom armoire. Even though she had to work quickly, she was fairly certain that she'd covered everything by the time she headed for Hanes's apartment ten minutes later. It had been a disappointing search. No better than the last batch of useless mail she'd snatched. She'd figured the police had already picked up anything of importance. But sometimes they overlooked a scrap that turned into a lead for her. Although what she'd really wanted to find was the name of the person who leased Sands the apartment. Hard to believe that anyone would pay rent for more than a year in advance.

It was Nick who let her in after she rang Hanes's doorbell. "Find anything?" he murmured as she walked past him.

"Nada."

"Figures."

She ignored his told-you-so tone and headed for the older man sitting on a faded plaid couch in the sparsely furnished living room, a tray of tea and biscuits in front of him.

"Did you get everything?" Hanes asked, his hands unsteady as he passed her a cup and saucer.

"I think so. Thank you." She sat with her tea and took a small sip while Nick settled in beside her. "You know, Mr. Hanes, I didn't know Dylan had a brother."

His disapproving frown reminded her to speak of

Sands in the present tense. "Dylan doesn't like to talk about his family." His faded gray eyes drifted toward Nick. "He claims they're all dead, but I think he may have had a falling-out with them."

According to what Taryn had found, there really was no family. "What makes you think that?"

A thoughtful frown creased his face. "Just a feeling, I guess."

"So, you don't actually know about a brother?"

He'd just leaned over to get a cube of sugar, but stopped to stare at her through narrowed eyes.

Taryn cringed inwardly. She sounded like a detective. Maybe she ought to just tell him the truth and hope he wasn't turned off by her initial deceit. "I'd feel horrible if he does have family and I made no effort to contact them after..." She let her voice trail off and tried to look sheepish.

Hanes finished dropping two cubes of sugar into his tea. Then he added a little milk. "Don't worry yourself. I may be wrong. Dylan treated me like a father, bringing me groceries, making sure my utility bills were paid. I figured I was a kind of substitute, maybe even a way for him to make amends to someone." He sat back, his eyes a little misty. "Why else would he befriend an old man with nothing to give in return?"

He sat in silence for a moment with a faraway look on his face, clearly remembering better times with his friend. Then he made a harrumphing sound. "I hated when all those nosy policemen came snooping around his apartment. Made me so mad." He lifted his cane a short distance off the ground and waved it back and forth. "I wanted to kick the lot of them out on their rears. Imagine digging into a person's privacy like that. And Dylan is a private one. Even with me.''

Taryn said nothing. Good thing she'd kept her mouth shut about being a detective. Not that Hanes was being particularly helpful. Except she was curious about the way his gaze kept lingering on Nick. Did he still believe him to be Sands's brother? Or in his loneliness, was *he* looking for a substitute for Sands?

Nick finally spoke up and asked him another question about his orchids. Hanes's mood lightened immediately, and as he began chattering, she used the time to study Nick.

Maybe it was the way his face was turned at this particular angle, or the lighting, or the power of Hanes's suggestion, but damned if Taryn didn't see the likeness to Sands. Although their eye and hair coloring were different, they had the same jaw shape and skin tone. But if Nick were Sands's brother, it didn't make sense for him not to be up front about it. Unless they *were* estranged, and Sands wanted nothing to do with Nick.

She pressed two fingers to her right temple to ease the building pressure. Too many sleepless nights lately. She needed a day off, and she needed to see Lucy.

''Do you have a headache, dear?'' Hanes peered at her with concern. ''I do have some pain powder.''

She lowered her hand. ''Sometimes the heat gets to me.'' She took another sip of tea, then placed the cup and saucer back on the tray. ''We really have to be going now, but I appreciate the tea and you letting me into Dylan's place.''

She and Nick both stood at the same time. Relying

on his cane, Hanes took a little longer to get to his feet, ignoring their offer to show themselves out.

"Well, I'm just glad you found all your belongings," he said as he followed them to the door. "I just grabbed as many things as I could before those nosy police started sniffing around."

Taryn and Nick had just stepped into the hall, and quickly exchanged glances. Nick had been oddly quiet, but now he looked as though he were about to say something. She cut him off. "You withheld some of Dylan's possessions from the police?"

"Withheld, my foot." The old man made a grumpy face. "Rescued, young lady. I rescued whatever I thought was important. Photographs, personal papers."

Dammit. Dammit. Dammit. No wonder the place seemed so clean. She looked helplessly at Nick. There wasn't a thing they could do to get a look at the removed items without arousing suspicion.

"Well…" Her thoughts scrambled for a solution. None came. "Thanks again, Mr. Hanes."

"Stop in for tea anytime," he said, lifting a wrinkled hand in farewell. "Or to visit my orchids."

"Maybe we'll do that. Goodbye." She waited until they got a ways down the hall before she muttered a curse under her breath.

"You get no argument from me." Nick's shoulder brushed hers, inflaming her irritation.

"Yeah? Since when?" She stabbed at the elevator button. "You find out anything from him?"

"Uh, let's see. He's a retired, widowed engineer who used his entire savings to buy that particular apartment because it faces the right direction for his greenhouse. Oh, and he's lived there for eleven years."

She gave him a bland look, then punched the button again. "About Sands?"

"Only that he kind of took the old man under his wing. Made sure he was eating more than canned goods, or didn't skimp on air-conditioning to save on the electric bill. That sort of stuff."

The elevator doors opened, and as they got in, she frowned. "Ten years is a long time to have that kind of relationship with someone and then disappear. Sounds like Hanes is like family."

"Yeah, but sometimes you hear of guys leaving their wife and kids without a word so they can start a new life."

"But don't you think it's strange that Hanes so adamantly believes Sands is coming back?"

Nick didn't answer. She turned to look at him and realized how close they were, and that he was watching her. Not just idly staring, but really focusing, the effort so intense she felt enveloped by him, his seductive scent tempting a primal urge that ignored good sense. The sudden desire to shrink into the corner of the car made her stand taller.

"I don't think it's strange at all," he finally said, and she had no idea what he was talking about. She'd lost the thread of their conversation the moment she felt the caress of his gaze. "He's a lonely old man and he wants to believe his friend will come back."

She breathed deeply, glad to be back on track. "You're sounding pessimistic. As though you're starting to think Sands is dead, or has vanished for good."

"Not at all. I'm just pointing out that Archie's reaction isn't strange under the circumstances."

She arched a brow. "Archie, huh?"

"I'm on a first-name basis with him *and* his orchids."

Taryn laughed, and he looked at her in that oddly intense way again. What had him so pensive? Was he holding back something he'd found out? Or was this about her? She shifted her purse between them.

The corner of his mouth lifted slightly. "On the other hand, he may know something about where Sands is."

"He was awfully concerned about protecting his things from the police," she noted as they left the elevator.

He let out a huff of air. "But everything is still speculation."

At the hint of disgust in his voice, she was tempted to remind him that she'd just been on the case two days, but the thought was as stifling as the humid Houston air engulfing them as they stepped out into the afternoon sun. Seemed more like months since she'd met him. And for God's sake, she'd already seen him naked. Or nearly so. But she couldn't think about that right now. It was hot enough.

"You are going to give me a ride?" Nick asked, following her to her car.

"Your hotel is downtown and it's rush hour."

For the first time since leaving Hanes's apartment he seemed more like himself, his grin smugly tolerant, and she seriously thought about leaving him behind. He hovered at the passenger door but didn't open it. "We'll have more time to talk."

"Oh, good," she muttered sarcastically. Louder she said, "Get in before I change my mind."

"I might even buy you dinner again." He immediately reached for the radio's volume control when she started the car.

"No dinner. I'm busy tonight."

"Your date can't reschedule?"

"You can either walk, or wait an hour for a cab."

"Okay." He held up his hands in supplication. "No more remarks from me. Just drop me off."

She smiled to herself. If she wasn't seeing Lucy tonight, she'd probably give in and have dinner with him. Which would be a totally unwise thing to do. Because she was starting to like Nick. Not that she wouldn't shoot down any notion he might have of following her around tomorrow. If she was going to make any headway on this case, it would be working alone.

She didn't have to worry, though. Good to his word, he didn't bring up anything to annoy her. In fact, he fell into a preoccupied silence that made her edgy. Made her think he knew something important she didn't.

He did speak a couple of times during the thirty minutes it took to get downtown, but nothing to get excited about. Which was fine because it gave her a chance to organize her thoughts for tomorrow. Priscilla Racine was going to get an early visit, which Taryn had decided not to let Nick in on. In fact, she'd decided not to tell him about the answering machine message.

Bumper-to-bumper traffic lined the street his hotel was on, and Nick offered to hop out two blocks away so she could take the next turn. It was so hot outside she started to refuse his suggestion, but he was out of the car before she could say a word.

She watched him walk down the street, and couldn't shake the notion that he was up to something. By the time she'd moved three car lengths, he'd already made it to the hotel.

Taryn sighed, turned down the air conditioner, the radio volume up, and cursed the traffic. She'd wanted to run home and grab a shower before seeing Lucy. That didn't seem likely now.

Five minutes later, cars finally started moving and she looked into her side mirror, hoping for a break to change lanes when she heard the passenger door open. "Nick?"

"Just drive," he said, anger darkening his face as he jumped in. "But don't go anywhere you'd normally go."

Chapter Nine

"What the hell is going on?" Taryn saw an opening between a Jeep and Mercedes and took it.

"Where were you headed?" he asked, and when she didn't answer, he said, "Wherever it was, don't go there. In fact, no place routine."

Fear coiled in her stomach. She was supposed to see Lucy. "Nick, if you don't tell me what's going on, I'm going as far as the next block, period."

He remained silent, and there was so much traffic on all sides to maneuver that she could only spare him a fleeting glance. Enough to see that he was angry. Furious. But he seemed worried, too.

"Nick, you're scaring me. What's happening?"

He let another stretch of silence lapse before he said, "Let's just get somewhere safe and I'll explain everything."

She wanted to demand he do it now, but she knew better. He had that preoccupied look, as if trying to sort something out, between frequent glances in his side mirror. And she had enough on her plate, trying to get out of this damn traffic mess.

The congestion eased up within minutes, and after several turns, she pulled up in front of Myron's Place.

It took Nick a moment to realize they had stopped, and when he saw where they were he swore. "I told you no place routine."

"I don't come here that often, weekends mostly. Besides, if there's going to be trouble, I know a lot of guys in here who would love to get in on the fun."

"I don't like it. This isn't smart."

"Well, if I knew what was going on, I might agree with you. But since I don't..." She'd already started getting out of the car.

He got out and followed her, cursing under his breath again, his sharp gaze scanning the street on either side.

She'd never admit it, but he was making her really nervous. There was a pent-up fury radiating from him that was foreign to her experience with him. Anger made a person do stupid things sometimes.

The place was crowded just as she expected it to be at this time of day. She waved to a couple of bikers she sometimes played pool with, spotted several other guys she knew as well. Fortunately, Moose was behind the bar and she breathed a sigh of relief. He was staring up at the television set he'd had installed a few months ago, his attention totally consumed. She glanced up to see what had caught his eye.

Harrison Cain's picture was plastered across the screen.

She squinted in disbelief, and as she neared the bar the television became audible. He'd been found murdered—tortured, then strangled—just thirty minutes ago. It had to have happened shortly after she'd met with him. She tried to swallow, but her mouth was so dry it wouldn't work.

So that's what Nick had been so upset about. She

turned to him, furious that he hadn't told her immediately, but he was still a few feet behind, his keen gaze sweeping the room until it collided with hers.

"You bastard."

His eyes narrowed on her, then shifted to the television. A stunned look crossed his face and he staggered back a step. He couldn't seem to tear his gaze from the screen as his shock bled into fury. It darkened his face, sparked fire in his eyes. It made the hair on the back of Taryn's neck stand on end.

"Get in the back room," he said in a low, harsh voice.

She nodded, willing to believe now that he hadn't known about Cain. She motioned to Moose, and when he saw her, he grinned.

"Good to see you, kid. The first beer's on me," he said, and reached for a mug.

"No, thanks, Moose. Look, I need your back room."

His expression sobered and he glanced briefly at Nick. "Trouble?"

"I don't think so, but we need to be invisible while we regroup."

He gestured with his chin. "No one's back there. You got the place to yourselves."

"Thanks." She started to turn and stopped. "Anyone you don't know comes in, you tell us, okay?"

"You got it. I'll stick close." He glared at Nick in warning as they headed for the back room.

Nick kept a watchful stance until they safely entered the room. He didn't blame the guy for being protective of Taryn. Some time today, Nick had become a hazard to her. He'd reconsidered going to Cain's Imports with her and made up that lame excuse for missing the appointment, but it didn't matter. They knew who he was, or just maybe, if he were damn lucky, they merely thought he was someone who could lead them to Sands. But it was clear by the message they'd left for him at the front desk of the hotel that they knew Nick was involved.

Dammit. How the hell had they found out? He'd been so careful. The news report had indicated Harrison had been beaten. But Nick knew the man well enough to know that he hadn't given Nick up. Harrison would have died first.

And he had.

A fierce anger skewered by grief pierced his composure and he slammed his palm down on the pool table. Pain shot up his arm. He didn't even flinch. Reluctantly, he looked over at Taryn, and guilt dealt a swift blow.

She stood on the other side of the pool table, watching him, mistrust and hostility written across her face. He deserved them both. "You ready to tell me what's going on?"

It wasn't a request. The hard edge to her tone said this was the end of the line for her. He truly wished it were. He'd fire her if he could, get her away from this deadly mess. But they knew who she was, and probably knew she could lead them to him. Once she did, she'd end up like Harrison.

The thought of his boss, tortured, strangled, brought a wave of fresh pain. But Nick's grief would have to wait. Harrison at least knew what the stakes were to this dangerous game he and Nick had orchestrated. Taryn hadn't. She was innocent. Just a woman trying to make a living. Now it was up to Nick to protect her.

"I'm waiting." Taryn had folded her arms across her chest, but her tone was lighter and the almost sympathetic look on her face made him wonder what kind of emotions he'd let slip.

Grief, anger, guilt—he couldn't afford any of those emotions right now. He still had to be careful about what he told her. He ran both hands through his hair, still feeling the sting in the one hand. "There's more to the story than I told you."

She uttered a short, startled laugh. "No kidding."

He shrugged, his mind still scrambling for the least-incriminating version of the truth to give her. When it was apparent that he was taking too long, she spoke up again.

"Is this about drugs?" she asked, continuing to keep her distance.

"No," he said in all honesty. "Absolutely not."

"Some kind of smuggling?"

He shook his head.

"Why am I doing all the talking here?" A hint of fear shadowed her impatience. "Who is Dylan Sands? And what does that import company really do?"

He rubbed the side of his jaw in frustration. "It's not really important."

"The hell it isn't."

"You're better off not knowing."

"Fine." She picked up the bag she'd left on the pool table. "I'm off the case. Have a nice life."

He grabbed her arm before she made it to the door. She tried to twist away, but he held her firmly, drawing her closer to maintain a better hold, until he had her pressed against his chest.

"It's not that simple, Taryn. They know who you are. They know where your office is."

She stopped struggling. Her pupils dilated, the black dominating the blue of her eyes. More curiosity than fear lurked in their depths. "Who?"

"I can't tell you that."

She tried to jerk away again without success. "Give me one good reason why I should stick around."

"To save that pretty neck of yours."

She didn't even blink. "The truth might help."

He could tell her part of it. If his mission was successful, it wouldn't matter what she knew. Alpha Agency would be disbanded. The guilty party imprisoned.

And if he wasn't successful? Chances were it still wouldn't matter. To either of them.

Her face was close, and so damn familiar. He'd been a fool to hire her in the first place. He'd felt the attraction immediately. Spending time with her had made it grow.

He took a deep breath. "Okay—"

A loud boom coming from the bar cut him off. Then came a couple of raised voices and the sound of splintering wood.

Taryn looked uncertain. "Fights aren't unusual around here."

The sound of the door opening drew their attention. Moose stuck his head inside. "Some jerk-off is looking for Dylan Sands, and he ain't being polite about it. I already called the cops, but you know how anxious they are to come to this neighborhood. Use the back door."

"He give you his name?"

"No."

"Thanks, Moose. I'll pay for any damages," Taryn

said as Nick dragged her toward the back door. The last thing he needed was to get the cops involved.

Moose glared at him. "Not a hair on her head. You got me?"

Nick nodded grimly, stepped outside, looked both ways down the alley, then pulled her along with him.

"We're going the wrong way," she said, and twisted free.

"We can't risk taking your car. We'll get a cab."

"At this hour? Good luck."

"Then we'll take a bus."

"Where are we going?"

He stopped when they got to the end of the alley, holding a restraining arm out so she wouldn't step out into the open yet. Then he casually peered around both corners.

She waited with an impatient sigh. "Sure would help if I knew who we were hiding from."

"Believe me. I'd give my left arm to know." He strained to see against the setting sun's glare and the frenzy of cars and people trying to get home after the workday. "Okay, let's go. There's a bus coming down the street on the left. We'll head for it slowly."

They'd made it almost a block when he noticed the lime-green sports car parked illegally. "Maynard," he muttered, nodding his head. "I was hoping it was that bastard."

"What? Where's Maynard?"

He glanced over his shoulder. No sign of the man. "That's his car." He gestured with his eyes toward the vehicle.

"There's got to be more than one green sports car in the city." Her gaze was watchful, scanning the sidewalk on both sides.

''That lime-green color? Look.'' He tugged at her arm. ''That cab's dropping off a fare. Let's try and grab it.''

It didn't appear the driver saw Nick trying to flag him down, so they raced across the street and nearly got sideswiped by the cab. They got in despite the driver's muttered profanities, and Nick told him to head for the Katy Freeway.

''Where are we going?'' Taryn asked, checking out the street behind them.

''There are some motels along the Katy.''

She sank back in her seat and stared at him. ''I'm not going to a motel. With you.''

''Don't worry. Your virtue is safe with me.'' He caught the mutinous set of her mouth before he turned to stare out the window, glad that remark had shut her up. At least temporarily. A lot was going on in his head. Like who else he'd jeopardized because of his arrogance. Archie? Priscilla?

What had made him think he could beat the odds? The message that had been left for him at the hotel had been succinct. And right on target. *Nobody leaves the agency.* He was told that from the very beginning. The same day they'd recruited him. But he'd been too arrogant to believe that applied to him. Harrison had warned him that it wouldn't be easy to defect. Now Harrison was lying on a slab.

He glanced over at Taryn. She was facing the window. Even her profile was perfect. What a beauty. How she'd gotten into this rotten business he'd never figure out. Every male head had turned her way when they'd walked into the restaurant last night, but she hadn't seemed to notice. She didn't use her looks like many women did. She was more concerned about her job, and sticking to her principles.

She hadn't been ready to give Sands up for any amount of money. Nick had no doubt she would have walked away from the case if he hadn't agreed that Sands could have final say on whether they'd meet. He admired that kind of integrity, that kind of respect for another human being. There was too much greed in the world already. It had gotten Harrison killed.

He hoped it didn't get Taryn killed, too.

The thought sliced through him with the deftness of a machete. Thinking about her getting hurt at all made his blood run cold. He shouldn't feel this way about her. Couldn't afford to. Perspective was what he needed. To remember the end result. This wasn't just about him. So many lives were involved.

They hit the Katy Freeway and Nick instructed the driver to head west of the city. A few miles later, a string of motels came into view. They got off at the next exit and Nick selected one of the more upscale establishments.

Taryn had remained quiet and watchful during most of the ride and while he checked them in under a false name. He was glad she wasn't asking more questions. Not that he thought she would let up. But he hadn't entirely planned how much he was going to tell her.

As soon as they entered the room, she eyed the two double beds. "Tell me you're not planning on spending the night here."

He opened the burgundy-and-gray floral drapes a little, glanced across the nearly empty parking lot, then immediately went to the television and flipped it on. "Probably." He checked his watch. "Is there any more news on after six?"

"I don't know. I don't watch the tube." She paced the modest-size room a couple of times. "I could call one of my buddies at the police station and find out the particulars on what happened to Cain."

He thought about it for a moment. The agency had long arms. The fewer phone calls they made the better. "Not yet. There can't be much information gathered to help us. Let's see what we can get from the TV." He paused. "What about a newspaper? Do they have an afternoon delivery here?"

She started to shake her head but straightened instead. Her gaze flickered to the right. "I think so. There was a machine outside the lobby. I could go check."

There was no longer afternoon delivery in Houston. He knew that. According to her body language, so did she. Damn, he was hoping he could trust her. The irony of that hypocrisy didn't elude him, and he exhaled sharply. "I just realized there wasn't enough time to make it to print today. Besides, it's really important that we stick together. No side trips. No phone calls. Understood?"

Anger brought color to her cheeks, and her eyes flashed fire. "And I'm supposed to follow you around like a good, meek little girl without benefit of an explanation? Think again, pal."

He half laughed, half grunted, and some of her anger was replaced with curiosity. She blinked warily at him. He rubbed the side of his jaw, weariness beginning to set in. "I wouldn't presume to think that for a single second." Her strength was something else he admired about her. Sighing, he said, "Harrison Cain was my boss."

Her expression slid from wariness to disbelief to confusion. She frowned and started shaking her head. "But...I don't...why..." She sank to the edge of the bed and sat hunched. "Are you really looking for Dylan Sands?"

He nodded.

"Cain wanted him, too?"

"Yes."

She narrowed her gaze. "Why the pretense? Why didn't he just hire an investigator himself?"

"He didn't want anyone else to know he was looking for Sands, or that Harrison even thought Sands might still be alive."

Still frowning, she chewed on her lower lip. "Why?"

Nick raked a hand through his hair and paced toward the window. This is where it got tricky. He stared out at the freeway and watched the steady stream of cars rush toward the city. "Harrison suspected that one of the guys who worked for him was into something underhanded and was using the company and his trips abroad as a cover."

"Sands?"

"No." He snorted. "Believe it or not, he's one of the good guys."

"So what does he have to do with all this?"

"He was investigating for Harrison—" Thinking about his mentor brought a lump to his throat and he had to pause and take in some air. *Dammit, Cain.* He swallowed. "When he disappeared."

She let a brief silence lapse, as if she understood

the pain of his loss. He was grateful. Too bad he couldn't tell her the truth.

"But you still think he's alive?" she asked. "Or is this about revenge?"

"No revenge." He turned away from the window and looked at her. "We just want to know what happened. And...we were hoping to make someone nervous by you asking questions. Looks like we succeeded."

She still looked unconvinced, even though he'd told her more of the truth than he'd planned. After leaving the edge of the bed, she walked up to the window and stood beside him but kept her gaze in the direction of the freeway. That didn't fool him. She was monitoring his reaction. "Why did you wait so long to look for him?"

"We tried once before. But no luck."

"Why didn't you get the police involved?"

He shrugged. "I'm sure Harrison had his reasons. Maybe he just didn't want his company dragged through the mud."

"Or he was dirty, and didn't want to risk uncovering anything he couldn't explain."

Before she barely got the last word out, Nick slammed his hand against the wall. "Harrison Cain was one of the most honorable men I have ever met."

Taryn didn't even flinch. "Maybe. But if you don't expect me to have questions, or to speculate on what the hell is going on, you're nuts."

He took a deep, even breath, then exhaled slowly. She was right, of course. "I don't know what Harrison's reasons were. I trusted the man, so I did as he asked."

She remained silent a long time, but he knew she

had a host of questions. Most of them he wouldn't be able to answer. "I have to make a phone call."

That he hadn't expected. "To whom?"

"It has nothing to do with the case."

"I'd prefer you didn't."

"Tough." She turned away and scooped her purse off the bed.

"Where are you going?"

"To the bathroom." She stopped to give him a taunting look. "If that's all right with you."

"Actually…" He lunged forward and grabbed her purse. "It's not."

Stunned at first, she just stood there, her eyes wide with disbelief. And then she rushed him.

Too late. He'd already removed her cell phone. He tossed the purse back to her.

She caught it with one hand, flung it on the bed, then continued to advance on him. "Give me my phone."

"You can't use it. You'll be traced."

She stood toe to toe with him, her warm breath caressing his chin. "I want the phone returned now." She said each word slowly, articulately.

Holding it away from her, he slipped out the battery and stuffed it into his jeans' pocket. "Here," he said, handing her the phone.

Murder flared in her eyes before her gaze skittered to his pocket. She could try, but she'd never be able to retrieve the battery.

She was still close. Close enough that he could smell the vanilla scent in her hair, feel her body heat, and he had to force himself to concentrate on his objective.

"Don't make me hurt you," she said, her eyes

fiercely blue and dead serious, and he had to stop himself from smiling.

It was probably true that she could take most men. Not him. He'd been trained too well. By the best. To be one of the elite few. But she didn't know that.

He thought five more seconds about his response, and again arrogance nudged him.

Before she could anticipate his next move, he grabbed both her wrists, propelling her none-too-gently backward, shoving her against the bed. Her knees buckled and he easily laid her back.

Immobilizing her, he covered her body with his.

Chapter Ten

"You were saying?"

If Taryn had her gun, she'd be tempted to shoot him. Nothing fatal. Maybe just a shot in the fanny. Enough to wipe that smug look off his face.

But there was another way.

For a few seconds she lay very still, then she tried to raise her shoulders off the bed. He quickly pinned her down again, just as she'd expected him to do.

She coughed, gasped for air, and coughed again.

"Nice try." He snickered. "You really expect me to fall for that?"

She coughed and gasped some more, throwing her head to the side, until she knew she was turning red in the face.

"Taryn?" The concern in his voice was her cue.

She jackknifed her body forward. He was too quick, and swiftly propelled her back to the mattress.

Taryn's breath left her lungs with a whoosh. Mostly from surprise, although he had her really pinned down. Flat enough that she couldn't even bring her knee up to do some damage.

"You made your point," she muttered through gritted teeth. "Get off."

He didn't answer and she couldn't see his face. A mixed blessing. Because he couldn't see hers, either. Couldn't see the desire building in her eyes as his hard chest crushed her breasts, her heart pounding wildly against him.

"Get off," she said again, this time bucking once.

He hardly moved, and all she managed to do was to cause more friction against her breasts. She was tempted to buck again.

"Are you going to cooperate?" His voice was low and gravelly, his breath drifting erotically down the side of her neck and raising goose bumps on her skin. His grip of one of her wrists loosened slightly as he started to prop himself up on his left elbow.

She made the barest of moves and he came down hard on her again, his chest pressed to hers, his hips pushing hers into the mattress. She lay perfectly still, shoring her breath, and felt his sex growing thick and hard against her belly.

Her breathing shut down altogether. Seconds later she gasped for air.

Nick pulled back to look at her, his eyes glittering dangerously. And then his gaze fell to her mouth, lowered to the rise and fall of her breasts. Slowly, he made his way back up to her face, his expression one of such hunger, her pulse rocketed.

He wasn't restraining her any longer. Not so that she couldn't escape, anyway. But she couldn't seem to move. She only stared back at him, her gaze helplessly caught in a web of longing and desire, her skin tingling with an awareness that defied every common-sense rule she lived by.

Abruptly, he sat up, his expression wary…almost grim. Although he continued to straddle her, he was obviously trying to put distance between them. Both physically and emotionally.

Hurt nudged her at first. Until she saw the tenderness in his eyes, the protectiveness, the concern. It stole her breath again. She blinked, swallowed. She felt like hitting him. Instead, she turned her face away so he couldn't see any sign of vulnerability.

"Taryn?" He lightly touched her chin with his fingertips and applied a small amount of pressure, trying to make her face him again.

"Don't."

"You know I wasn't going to really hurt you," he said softly.

She almost laughed. Maybe not physically. "Okay, you proved you're stronger. You can get up now."

"Taryn?" His voice was probing but gentle, compassionate, and she couldn't take it another moment.

Catching him off guard this time, she jerked up and sent him sprawling backward. He would have landed on the floor except for his lightning-quick reaction, and instead ended up flat on his back in the center of the bed.

"Surprise can overcome superior strength," she said with a smug tilt of her head. "You should know that."

She started to slide off the quilt and made it as far as the edge when he manacled her wrist and dragged her back. She tried to twist away, but he yanked her toward him. With her right hand, she braced herself from falling face-first onto his chest. But that left her with an arm slung around him, his mouth so close to hers, she wondered if hitting face-first wouldn't have been better.

"I do know," he said in a menacingly even tone. "Harrison drummed that into me."

Even though his expression didn't waver, she felt the pain radiating from him. The mournful look in his eyes when he'd talked about his boss earlier would forever be etched in her mind.

She released a slow breath and relaxed her tensed muscles. "I'm sorry about your friend."

Distrust flitted across his features, as though he thought this might be a diversionary tactic. But then he also started to relax, and when she slumped against him, he loosened his hand around her wrist and lightly touched her cheek.

"I hope I didn't frighten you," he said, stroking the sensitive skin around her ear.

A slow, wry smile curved her lips. Oh, he scared the hell out of her, all right. But not how he thought he had. Not by pinning her down, or grabbing her arms or even kissing her. He'd done far worse. He'd touched her soul, reminded her of her woman's heart. Damn him.

"Why did you come get me?" she asked suddenly.

Stilling his hand, he frowned. "When?"

"After I dropped you off at the hotel, you could have taken off when you realized everything was going to hit the fan. Why did you..." Her voice trailed off as another thought occurred to her. She was his only link to him. Had he ditched her, he would have been in the clear while she led the parade in another direction. In a way he'd risked his life for her. She swallowed hard.

"Taryn?" He touched her cheek again.

She'd been staring at him, but not really seeing. He came into focus now, his eyes that dark shade of concern, and she felt her protective wall begin to crumble. How long had it been since someone had taken care of her?

Yes, he'd lied to her from the start, and she was still peeved about that, but when it had really counted, Nick had been there for her. And right now, she didn't give a damn about anything except feeling his naked body comforting hers.

''Are you okay?'' He picked up her trembling hand and sandwiched it between his warm palms.

She nodded, a short jerky movement that had him frowning deeper. He started to speak again, but she put a finger to his mouth to silence him.

She moistened her dry lips, then cleared her throat, feeling awkward suddenly. He waited, mutely, his wary gaze roaming her face, and at the thought of her unnerving him, a giggle bubbled in her chest. It gave her the boost of confidence she needed, and she fisted the front of his shirt and pulled him toward her before he guessed her intention.

Their lips met clumsily at first, mostly due to his surprise, and then the hunger took over, consuming them, driving them into a frenzy. Adrenaline made the blood race like wildfire through her veins. Nick had caught the fever, too. She'd seen it in his darkened eyes, heard it in his ragged breathing, could taste his recklessness.

When he started unfastening the buttons of her blouse, she didn't hesitate to reach for his. The intensity, the urgency with which they pulled off each other's clothes was almost frightening. Except this was Nick. He hadn't abandoned her when she'd needed him. Her parents had, in the name of pride. So had Derek, in the name of greed.

She wouldn't allow herself to be fooled by Nick's attentiveness, though. It would only be this one night. And that's all she wanted. To satisfy a physical craving. To ease the flow of adrenaline.

Taryn had already seen him naked. Well, almost naked. The last two nights her imagination had filled in the rest. But her imagination was sorely lacking.

Nick was truly beautiful. Perfectly proportioned. Toned. Muscled, but not too bulky. Except where it really counted, and that was okay with her.

She watched him toss their clothes on a chair, ignoring that half of them missed the mark, and when he turned back to her, she had to force herself to take a deep, steadying breath. Never had she seen so much intense desire in a man's face as when his gaze connected with hers, held it, caressed it, captured it. Then it lowered to her mouth, lingering for a moment before falling to her bare breasts.

Her nipples were hard and anxious, and his nostrils flared slightly at the recognition. When he looked back at her face, he smiled, a slightly sensual curve of his lips that warmed her to her core.

He anchored both of his hands around her waist and pulled her toward him. He wasn't all that gentle, but the tenderness had never left his eyes and Taryn had never felt more safe or sure in her life.

''This wasn't supposed to happen,'' he whispered, and then sighed deeply when their bodies made contact, skin to skin, heat to heat.

His warm breath swirled around her ear, his beard-roughened chin grazed her shoulder. She closed her eyes and let her head fall back. Nick kissed the curve of her jaw, the side of her neck before lowering his mouth to her breasts.

She clutched his shoulders, her nails digging into his flesh as he teased her nipples. His muscles were tensed and knotted, and she sensed it was the restraint he was exercising that was the cause. Pent-up energy radiated from him, infusing her fingertips with a restlessness, urging her to explore.

That would be tricky. If he wasn't supporting her at her waist, she might not be able to continue standing. So she nudged him toward the bed.

He needed little encouragement. Their bodies still wrapped around each other's, he centered them on the queen-size mattress, his movements swift, almost desperate. She understood his urgency, felt the same need to comfort and connect. Adrenaline. That's all it was.

He pulled away, and the loss she experienced was frighteningly immediate. But then his eager mouth tasted her breasts again, and she briefly closed her eyes in relief, and helpless gratitude.

When his tongue traced a route down her belly, Taryn moaned and reached for him. She'd barely felt the tip of his silky-smooth manhood when he moved out of reach. She writhed in protest, but he ignored her, parted her thighs, and then she felt his mouth on her again.

Her climax came startlingly fast. Arching off the bed, she clutched the quilt as the spasms hit at amazing speed and intensity. Her moans fueled Nick and his mouth grew hotter and more eager until she had to finally twist away.

He kissed a path along her hip, up the side of her breast. "Don't tell me you've had enough," he said, his voice ragged against her neck.

She had him right where she wanted him, and she spread her legs again. "What do you think?" she whispered as she pulled him down and he slipped inside her.

TARYN ROLLED OVER TO LOOK at Nick lying on his side, his eyes closed, his arm slung around her, and knew she was in trouble. Making love with him had nothing to do with adrenaline.

That annoying little flutter that started in her belly and migrated to her chest was back. Damn him. She lifted a hand and brushed a lock of dark hair off his forehead. He opened his eyes.

"Hey." A lazy smile tilted the corners of his mouth. "I guess I fell asleep." He stretched out his back, while letting his palm roam over her bare bottom. "How about you?"

"For about fifteen minutes. You were only out for twenty." Already she felt the stirrings of arousal triggered by his light touch. But she wouldn't make love with him again. They had already done that twice. By the second time, she knew she was in deep. Her only chance to get her head back on straight would be to resume their old relationship as soon as possible.

Just as he ducked his head for a kiss, she raised herself to a sitting position, keeping the sheet stretched across her breasts and tucked under her arms. She glanced around the room, searching for her clothes, and did exactly what she didn't want to do. She looked at Nick.

He'd locked his hands behind his head, and lying back, he watched her, his expression suddenly grim. "What's going on in that head of yours, Taryn?"

She shrugged and scooted to the edge of the bed.

Damn, she wished she'd put her clothes on before he'd awakened. Without giving him another look, she got up and walked over to the chair where her bra dangled from the arm. On the floor were her panties, and she quickly pulled both articles on.

"Taryn?"

"You want the bathroom first?" she asked, still without looking at him.

"I want you to talk to me."

She sighed. "Everything is fine, Nick." She slipped on her shirt and turned around. He hadn't moved, but because she'd dragged the sheet with her, his portion barely covered his hips. She dragged her gaze away from his solid, broad chest, where she had laid her head only moments ago.

"Everything is fine," she repeated, her voice not quite as steady this time. "Really. It's just that I've got to make that phone call."

His expression changed from one of concern to annoyance, and he unlocked his hands to scrub his face, then jammed one through his hair. "We went over that already." He exhaled loudly. "Who do you need to call?"

She stiffened. She didn't want to tell him about Lucy. And yet she did. Except, two rounds of love-making didn't suddenly make Nick Travis trustworthy. He'd already lied to her. Besides, what they'd shared had only been sex. Nothing more.

Liar.

Turning away from him, she picked up her slacks. *Stupid. Stupid. Stupid.* Everything had changed this afternoon. Just as she'd known it would. But she'd been reckless, anyway, and now her objectivity had been compromised. "Not that I think it's any of your business, but I need to call a friend who I was supposed to meet in a half hour. If I don't show up she'll worry and start calling around.''

"Why the sudden attitude, Taryn? We're on the same side." He paused, and she could hear him leaving the bed. "Aren't we?"

"I don't know, Nick." She took a deep breath as she pulled on her slacks, then turned to face him. "Are we? Have you told me everything?"

He studied her for a minute, oblivious to his nakedness, and it took all her willpower to keep her gaze level with his. He maintained his silence as he reached for his boxers and jeans and pulled them on. When he'd gotten his zipper halfway up, he stopped and frowned at her. "This isn't about the case or what I did or didn't tell you. You regret making love."

She laughed. "We didn't make love. We had sex. Very good sex." Shrugging, she added, "Fantastic sex, actually. But that's all it was." She looked down and fidgeted with her own zipper before her eyes gave away her lie.

"You don't believe that." His voice was close.

Wary, she glanced up and he slid a hand around her nape and pulled her toward him. His mouth covered hers in a bruising kiss. And then it turned gentle, coaxing. God help her, she should have pushed him away but she didn't.

"Do you?" he asked against her mouth.

She stepped back, and he let his hand trail away from her. "It doesn't matter."

A knowing gleam entered his eyes. No smugness. Merely recognition. "Let's go make the call from across the street."

She was glad he'd dropped the subject, but no way

was he going to eavesdrop on her phone call. Lucy was going to remain Taryn's little secret, she'd decided, but it wasn't only that, there was principle involved. "I don't need a chaperone."

At her abrupt tone, he narrowed his gaze. "Why so defensive if you're only calling a friend?"

"Are we going to start comparing notes on who tells the truth around here?" She picked up her purse and gave him a sugary smile. "We both know who'd lose that contest."

Nick pursed his lips, his expression tolerant, as if she were a child who just didn't understand. Her blood pressure soared and she wove around him, headed for the door before she said something she'd regret.

He looped an arm around her waist and hauled her back. Anger sizzled in her veins. Mostly because of the way her body instantly responded to his touch.

"So help me God, Taryn, we're sticking together no matter what. I don't give a damn if you have to go to a gynecologist's appointment. You are not leaving my sight."

It wasn't so much the anger in his voice that stopped her, but the hint of fear, of desperation that seasoned each word like salted popcorn. He seemed genuinely uneasy, and she was tempted to give in, let him accompany her.

Except she absolutely couldn't tell him about Lucy. She didn't fear for her daughter's safety as far as Nick was concerned, but Taryn had already been stripped of most of her defenses. Her carefully constructed shell had been penetrated and she wasn't sure if she'd ever be able to crawl back inside. Lucy was her last and greatest vulnerability. Her Achilles heel. If Taryn could just hold on to that one small piece of herself, maybe she'd be okay when this was all over.

She dropped her purse and folded her arms across her chest. "Okay, finish telling me why you're so paranoid."

"Paranoid?" He shook his head in disbelief. "A man is dead, Taryn."

Briefly she closed her eyes, unwilling to see the pain on his face at the reminder. "I know," she whispered. "Believe me, I'm taking this situation seriously. But you're taking things too far. No one knows where we are. We can't be traced."

His laugh was without humor, short, bitter. "You don't know who you're dealing with. Weren't you a little surprised they knew about Myron's Place?"

"You're right. I don't know who I'm dealing with, or who *they* are. Because *you* haven't been honest with me. You're still hedging."

Nick knew she was furious. She had every right to be. He had misled her. And he would have to continue to do so.

Or he could trust her with the truth.

A couple of hours ago it had been a lot easier to look her in the eyes and deceive her. Not now. Not when he could still taste her. Not when her mysterious scent still swarmed his senses and coated his skin.

He raked a hand through his hair and paced away from her, toward the window, his gut constricting at the prospect of exposing himself, of becoming so infinitely vulnerable. Not just to her. To anyone. He'd worked too hard the past year, meticulously covering his tracks, enduring all the surgeries and impatiently waiting through the long period of recovery. He thought of all the months spent planning his escape. Plotting the execution of his final mission.

Taryn was damn good. As a bounty hunter, she had an over eighty-five percent recovery rate. He'd checked. And even she hadn't uncovered the truth. Now that he'd had time to think rationally, he wasn't so convinced the person who sent the message to his hotel knew who Nick was. Did he really want to give up his hard-won anonymity?

With a weary sigh, he turned away from the window and his gaze immediately collided with hers. Hurt, sorrow, regret clouded her blue eyes. She was tough, and she tried not to show any of it, but he'd wounded her, all right. And that knowledge was like a spear through his heart.

God, he hoped he didn't regret this.

"Okay, Taryn, you want the truth," he said, bracing himself and watching distrust alter her expression. "I'm Dylan Sands."

Chapter Eleven

Taryn stared at him in stunned silence. Nick was Dylan Sands. That didn't make sense.

Did it?

She tried to recall the photo she had of Sands, but she was feeling pretty dazed, almost like she'd had one too many beers. The hair color wasn't the same, she knew. Nick's was darker. And his eyes were brown, not hazel. But a drugstore tint and contact lenses could take care of both of those things.

Snippets of conversation rewound in her head. She recalled Nick's odd behavior around Archie Hanes. The old man's mistaking Nick for Sands's brother. More thoughts and recollections kept tumbling through her head.

Instinct had told her something wasn't right from the beginning. But she'd allowed her intuition, her most basic tool, to be undermined by her attraction to Nick...Dylan...hell, she didn't know what to call him now.

"I know you're ticked off, and I don't blame you," Nick said, and she realized she'd almost forgotten he was there. "But I couldn't compromise my identity. There's too much at stake."

He started to close the distance between them, and she stepped back, not ready to have him touch her. A sad, fleeting smile touched the corners of his mouth, and he took the chair that only a few minutes ago had been draped with their clothes.

"Aren't you going to say anything?" he asked when the silence had lengthened again.

She shrugged. "What do I call you? Dylan? Nick?"

A solemn expression was his only reaction to her flip tone. "Dylan Sands is dead. As far as you or anyone else is concerned. Or believe me, Nick Travis will be."

The cold detachment in his eyes made her shiver. "No one else knows?"

"Harrison did, of course." His shoulders slumped against the chair. "Now, only you."

She pressed her lips together, digesting the information. Had that knowledge gotten Harrison Cain murdered? Rubbing the back of her neck, she sat at the edge of the bed, facing him.

It was still hard for her to reconcile the photo of Dylan Sands with Nick, even knowing they were the same man. After Archibald Hanes had noticed the resemblance, she'd seen some of it herself, but it was amazing how much different he really looked.

She must have been staring for too long, because he finally said, "Surgery. Lots of it."

"I figured as much. Whoever did it did an incredible job." Fleeting bits of information about Sands added to the confusion in her head. Harrison Cain had called him a chameleon. No kidding. "You'd better start from the beginning."

He nodded ruefully. "This time I won't leave anything out."

She let out an inelegant snort. "At this point, that wouldn't be wise."

He stared at her, the regret on his face almost stifling. "I never meant to compromise you. I was arrogant. Once I knew I had covered my tracks well, I thought this was going to be a quick assignment." He shook his head. "You'll never know how sorry I am."

She knew. Enough that her anger was tempered with empathy. And fear. For him. She cleared her throat. "You forgot what I do for a living. It's a dangerous business with no guarantees."

He half smiled. "I don't deserve your charity."

"I know."

His gaze locked with hers for a long silent moment, and then he exhaled an expansive breath. "You were right about Cain's Imports. It's a front. For the government."

Taryn blinked, not expecting that claim at all. Was this another tall tale?

Obviously her skepticism showed, and he said, "I don't know how I can expect you to believe me now, but that's the truth."

"As in FBI or CIA?"

"Something like that. We have three cover offices in Houston, New York and San Francisco, with eighteen operatives. We're referred to as Alpha Agency, although few bureaucrats would acknowledge our existence. We work independently, on a need-to-know basis. I don't even know who Harrison reported to."

Again the coldness in his eyes unnerved her. And in the thick, tense silence he let lapse, she got the message. Cain's people were responsible for messy assignments. Despicable ones that would embarrass the government. Actions that would repulse her. She tried to show no reaction.

"I'd worked for them for about eight years when things started going sour. Canceled missions that were executed, anyway. Unaccountable car explosions when our guys were abroad. Harrison suspected one of our own had gone over the edge and turned vigilante. But we didn't know who."

She shook her head in disbelief. "So you went through all the surgery and changed your identity just to investigate?"

His expression turned wry. "I wish I were that noble. I wanted out of the agency and that was the only way."

"Sounds sinister."

"You don't know the half of it."

"Did Harrison blackmail you into this?"

He snorted. "No, he stuck his neck out for me. When I went to him about resigning he asked if I was crazy. Told me I should have known there was no way out. I was an agency man." His laugh sent another chill through her. "Until death did us part."

She shook her head, trying to process all this surreal information. "How did you get involved with them?"

"I was recruited out of the New York Police Department."

"You were a cop?"

"Why the surprise?" He stretched his neck from side to side. She could almost feel the restless energy building inside him, trying to escape, trying to ease itself. "I come from three generations of cops. If you were born male in my family, you became a cop. Period. No discussion.''

"What did they say about you departing from tradition and joining the agency?''

He shrugged. "None of my family know. Part of my deal was that no one knew where I was or what I was doing.''

She frowned. "You had to tell them something. You couldn't just disappear—'' The impassive look on his face stopped her. That's exactly what he'd done. Just disappeared. Was this a pattern with him?

"That was the only way I could join the agency. As far as my family, well, I was never the type of cop, or son, for that matter, they wanted. I wasn't like the rest of the boys in blue, drinking beer and playing poker on Friday nights, bowling on Saturdays. You might say I was my dad's biggest disappointment.''

Taryn's stomach tightened. He wouldn't want her sympathy, but he had it, anyway. She understood being the outcast all too well. "So, no goodbyes or anything.''

"Oh, yeah. I submitted my resignation, told the folks I'd taken a job as a private bodyguard in Mexico.'' He lifted a shoulder. "It was better we not have any contact after that. For their sake and mine. The people I do business with don't always play fair.''

His smile gave her a shiver. She thought about Lucy and all the precautions she'd taken to make sure her daughter would never become a bargaining tool, or a means to get to her or Derek. It was probably unnecessary paranoia, but it allowed Taryn to sleep at night.

"Where do your parents think you are?'' she asked,

aware that this wasn't something he wanted to talk about.

"Caught up in my own life. Or dead." His expression didn't waver, but something in his eyes made her think he wasn't so blasé as he pretended.

"That's why you adopted Archibald Hanes," she murmured, and when his displeased gaze met hers, she realized she'd spoken her thoughts out loud.

"Don't go there," he said curtly. "I don't need any psycho-babble from you."

"Hit a nerve, did I?"

He shoved an uneasy hand through his hair and gave her a warning look. "I'm worried about Archie. I'm not certain they know who I am, but if they do, they might use him to get to me."

"Everything you told me about him is true, then?"

His gaze narrowed. "In what respect?"

"You took him under your wing, made sure he had enough money, that sort of thing."

Shrugging, he looked away. "He spent every penny he had on that apartment in order to have his greenhouse. He made a lot of sacrifices. Hell, I don't have any heirs. It was no skin off my nose."

Taryn smiled. "You're a kind man, Nick."

"Yeah, right. Everyone puts their friends at risk."

"Don't jump to conclusions. You said yourself they might not have figured out who you are. Considering their line of work, this may not even be about you or whether they think Sands is still alive."

He looked abruptly at her, and she knew she'd given him something to think about. "You could be right," he said slowly. "But I doubt it." He got up and went to the window, pushed the drapes aside just a little and glanced around the parking lot before returning to his chair.

Taryn rubbed her arms. For all her rationale and brave talk, she was a little apprehensive. "You don't really think they know where we are."

He carefully studied her face. "As long as you haven't used the phone or told anyone."

She kept her gaze level with his and slowly shook her head. "No, but I really do have to make a call." She glanced at her watch. "Like…immediately."

"Must be important if you're willing to drop this conversation. Not that there's much more to it."

"I'm not willing to drop it. Not by a long shot. But I need to make this one call." Lucy expected her at any minute and Taryn wasn't about to not show up without an explanation. Besides, she didn't know when she'd be able to contact her again. She picked up her purse and withdrew her wallet. "I'll run across to the gas station and use the pay phone."

Nick immediately stood.

"You don't need to go with me. I'm just taking my wallet. Hell, I'll take only thirty-five cents if you want, and I'll be right back."

"I could use the walk," he said, his expression unyielding. "I need to stretch my legs."

"Look, Nick, I get it. These are really bad people. They probably have endless resources for tracking us, or getting information they want. I'm not going to do anything stupid."

"Then you won't mind if I go with you."

She let out a sound of exasperation. There was no need for him to know about Lucy, she'd decided. It wasn't that she didn't trust him; in fact, she probably owed him her life. She was even honored by the courage and extraordinary trust he'd possessed in her to reveal he was Sands. In spite of the fact that he'd put her in this situation. But she wasn't ready to trust him with her daughter's life. On that front, she trusted no one.

"I need to call Archie, too. Just to make sure he's all right."

She sighed, resigned. "Okay." She was going to have to call Moose, instead. Have him call Lucy. "Come on."

He was right behind her, shadowing her down the corridor to the elevator. When they got to the first floor and the doors slid open, he laid a hand on her arm and left the elevator first, casually looking both ways.

Uneasiness crawled over her skin like an army of ants. Initially she'd hoped he was overreacting. Now she knew better. "What's the plan?" she asked as she came up alongside him.

"Obviously I have to find out who killed Harrison." He glanced at her. "It would be easier on me if you left town until I do."

"Tough."

"That's what I thought."

"Anyway, there's no guarantee they wouldn't follow me."

"I can take care of that part."

The deadly certainty in his voice convinced her, made her eye him again. His face was a cold, hard mask. This was the dark side of Nick Travis of which she hadn't seen much, and another thought occurred to her. "What are you trying to do, make me a target again so that I'll flush them out?"

Color drained from his face and his gaze swung to

hers. The stricken look she saw in his eyes provided her answer. Then he startled her by pulling her into his arms. They'd made it to the lobby where a family of four pushed through the front door. Nick ignored their stares and held her close with one arm.

He lifted her chin with his free hand. There was a fierceness in his gaze that paralyzed her. "No. I do not want to make you a target. I want you safe."

Taryn held her breath, mesmerized by the sincerity in his eyes, the protectiveness she felt in his touch. She nodded, unable to speak. Glancing sheepishly at the gawking couple, she stiffened, and he slowly let her go.

She jerked away and pushed open the glass doors to the parking lot, and took in a lungful of sticky humid air. What the hell was happening to her? Why should she believe him now? Just because they'd had sex?

Except it hadn't been only the physical act of sex. They had made love, and she could deny it all she wanted but her heart knew better. She forced all emotion out of her head, out of her being. That weakness could get them both killed.

"Are you pretty convinced it's Maynard who's behind all this? The car near Moose's could have just looked like his," she asked, walking briskly across the parking lot toward the street.

He'd kept up with her, shooting her sidelong glances she wouldn't intercept. "I sure want it to be him. The guy's an ass, and you summed him up pretty well—a real loose cannon. But I can't let my feelings interfere. I can't overlook Cross. Or Syd."

"But you don't want it to be Syd."

His laugh was short, bitter. "I must be getting soft."

"For what it's worth, I don't think it's Syd, either."

They arrived at the intersection, and while they waited for the red light and traffic to dwindle, he stared at her. "Is this emotion or instinct talking?"

There was a caustic edge to his voice she hadn't heard before. It sounded suspiciously like he was jealous. "What do you mean?"

He shrugged. "Syd's a good-looking guy. Women are usually attracted to him."

A smile tugged at her mouth, but she pressed her lips together. "Yes, he is. But that's not what I'm basing my opinion on." She paused, recalling her conversation with Syd. "When I gave him the Jamaican fisherman story, I thought he reacted strangely."

Nick's abrupt laugh cut in, followed by a mild curse. "I can't believe you came up with that story. You have no idea how accurate you were."

The irony made her lips curve a little. "In retrospect, I think Syd may have figured out you broke away from the agency and staged the disappearance. And he seemed pretty damned pleased."

Nick's forehead furrowed in thought, but a smile softened his eyes. "Yeah, Syd would appreciate that. We sometimes shared our discontent, but I still can't ignore the fact that he was in nearby cities at the time of two unsanctioned assassinations."

Assassinations? Her gaze flew to his face, but he'd turned to check the traffic. Was that what Nick had done? Had he been an assassin for the government?

What exactly did he plan to do if he found Harrison's killer? A chill chased down her spine.

"What about people from the New York and San Francisco offices? Could they be involved?"

"Possibly. I can't prove they aren't. But according to the itineraries Harrison got his hands on, the operatives from those offices were accounted for or on other assignments when major…" He darted a glance at her, then looked away. "When things started happening." He grabbed her hand as the light changed to green and the traffic stopped.

She matched his long stride to the other side, and when they stopped at the pay phone, she hesitated. "We should call the police. There's a good chance I know the officer investigating Harrison's murder and—"

He was already shaking his head. "No way. I can't get them involved. I don't exist, remember?"

"But now they're looking for the same guy we are, and we're probably a hell of a lot closer than they are and—"

He grabbed both her arms. "Dammit, Taryn, don't you get it yet? We aren't dealing with the ordinary scum you usually chase down. These guys have a lot of muscle and power and resources behind them. Hell, I don't even know how far up the corruption goes. I have to stay dead. Or I will be."

She blinked, feeling the fight drain out of her. If she'd dreamed for one second that they had any chance of a future, all hope evaporated. An avalanche of doubt and fear shut down her ability to feel and she went numb. "What about me?"

His grip slackened and he moved his palms in a caressing motion up and down her arms. "I'm the one who knows too much. About the agency, the entire operation. From the moment they recruited me, they owned me. Harrison, the poor bastard, was dying from lung cancer and he still had no way out. Like the message they left me at the hotel said—no one leaves the agency.'' He gently squeezed her arms. ''You'll be okay after this is over.''

Would she? She jerked away and turned to the pay phone. At least he'd correctly interpreted her question. She would have died of humiliation if he'd thought she was considering the possibility of a future relationship. Which, of course, she was not.

She dug in her pocket for change. He held out a handful to her. She didn't want to take it for fear her hands would tremble. He finally fished out the correct amount and pressed the coins into her hand. Her palms were cold and damp.

''You don't have to stay in this business, Taryn. I have money. Lots of cash. You can leave Houston. Make a fresh start.'' His voice was urgent, his eyes a silent plea.

You can leave Houston. Not ''we.'' ''You're saying I'll still be in danger?''

''I'm saying you deserve better.''

She searched his face. Better than him? ''I need to make my call,'' she mumbled, and turned away.

She didn't know how she got her unsteady fingers to drop the coins in the slot, or to punch in Moose's number, but the phone started ringing and she forced herself to concentrate on what she could tell Moose without arousing Nick's suspicion.

After twelve rings no one answered. Obviously she'd dialed the wrong number, because Moose was always there. She tried again, letting it ring twenty times with no luck. By the third try, her heart hammered in her chest.

At her sharp intake of breath, Nick frowned. "What's wrong?"

"No one is answering at Moose's place."

He angled his watch, and she saw it was eight. "I assume that's unusual."

"He's always there. He should be slammed with customers about now." She pressed two fingers to her temple and briefly closed her eyes. Panicking would do no good.

"Maybe he's too busy to get the phone."

"I doubt it," she said, but dropped the coins in the slot again. She let it ring thirty times, her pulse speeding out of control. Something was wrong. She felt it in her gut.

"Try him at home."

"He lives above the bar. It's the same line." She took a deep breath. She had to call Lucy direct. Right now, she needed to hear her daughter's voice more than anything.

"Who are you calling now?" Nick asked, his voice tight.

Ignoring him, she finished pounding in the numbers while continuing to take deep, steadying breaths. She half expected him to try to disconnect the call, but he must have sensed her fear and stood quietly to the side.

Her heart in her throat, she waited through six rings. Seven. Eight. Someone had to be home. They were expecting her. And then she remembered the answering machine. It should have picked up after four rings.

"Oh, God, oh, God." She disconnected the phone

and started punching in the numbers again. This time more carefully. She was nervous. She'd probably gotten the wrong number, she told herself, not believing a word.

"Taryn, what is it?"

His voice sounded like an echo vibrating down a tunnel from far away. She had to get to Lucy. She had to know she was okay.

No answer.

She dropped the phone and ran for her car. She stared frantically at the empty gas station parking lot. Her car wasn't here. And then she remembered. It was still at Moose's.

"Taryn." Nick grabbed her roughly by the arm and swung her to face him. "What's wrong?"

"I have to get to Clear Lake."

"What are you talking about?"

"It's about forty-five minutes away."

"I know where it is." His grip tightened when she tried to pull away. "Why?"

"I've got to get a car." Her gaze darted to a pair of pickup trucks parked behind the station. It would take her about two minutes to hot-wire one.

"Taryn, calm down and tell me what's going on."

"I don't have time." She tried to twist away. He wouldn't let her.

"We'll rent a car, okay? I'll drive you to Clear Lake. Just tell me where exactly we're going."

Her mind stopped racing long enough so that she could focus on his face. Concern darkened his features. She wanted to slap the worried expression off. Something was wrong with Lucy, and it was his fault. She knew it way down deep where a mother has a sixth sense.

She tried to rein in her panic. A clear head. That's what she needed. She didn't care what Nick knew about her anymore. She just had to get to Lucy.

"I have to go to Clear Lake," she said, her breath catching. "And find my daughter."

Chapter Twelve

That Nick could keep his mind on his driving was a small miracle. Now they just needed one more, he thought as they sped south on the Gulf Freeway toward Clear Lake. Only divine intervention would prevent the agency, or Maynard, or Cross or whoever was behind this from knowing about Taryn's daughter.

He figured God had no use for the likes of him. But just might spare a little ten-year-old girl. An innocent child. Placed in harm's way because of Nick.

He spat a vicious curse, and from his peripheral vision, he saw Taryn turn to look at him. He didn't look back. He couldn't meet her eyes. Not after what he had done to her. And maybe her daughter.

"Get off at the next exit and turn right," she said, then angled her face to stare out the window.

She'd barely said a word for the past hour, the time it took to rent a car and get on the road. He had no idea what she was thinking, but he could guess. He doubted it would do any good to tell her he wouldn't have hired her had he known about Lucy. At least, he didn't think he would have. Because he honestly hadn't thought it would come to anything like this.

Had he?

He muttered another curse.

Damn, he didn't know. His desire for escape, for vengeance had been so great during the past year and a half, it had clouded his vision. In the murky light it was so easy to sell himself on self-righteousness, convince himself that the end justified the means, no matter how ruthless the quest. But something had changed in the past couple of days. Hell, he had changed. Maybe he'd finally sprung a conscience.

Maybe Taryn had opened his eyes.

"You'd better slow down," she said, "or you'll pass the street."

He let his foot off the accelerator and glanced at the speedometer. He looked into the rearview mirror. It was a wonder he hadn't been pulled over.

"Turn right here."

She sounded amazingly calm, but she hadn't stopped wringing her hands. He wanted to cover them with his own, still her, reassure her. But he wasn't welcome, and he didn't blame her.

Besides, reassuring her would be a lie. If her daughter had been taken, it was all over.

After they veered right, she didn't tell him to stop, just opened her door and ran toward a small square brick house. He jammed on the brake, threw the car in Park and ran after her.

The front door was open and even before they entered the house, Nick could see that the living room had been tossed, chairs turned over on their sides, cushions shredded. Anger ripped a path through him. No doubt they'd come to grab the girl. Any other violence was unnecessary.

"Olivia!"

Taryn's voice broke as she ran toward a thin, gray-ing woman in a torn blue dress huddled on the floor in the corner, her wrists and ankles bound with nylon rope, a filthy rag tied around her mouth. Her red-rimmed blue eyes were wide with fear. Tears streamed down her flushed cheeks.

Taryn knelt down beside the woman and untied the rag. "Where's Lucy?"

The woman sobbed uncontrollably. She looked to be in her late fifties, but it was hard to tell with her face puffy and swollen. She gasped for air a couple of times. "He t-took her," she said brokenly. "I couldn't d-do anything." She dissolved into hysteri-cal tears.

Taryn remained calm. Too calm. "It wasn't your fault, Olivia. There wasn't anything you could do," she said in a low, soothing tone while she untied the woman. "Did you get a look at him?"

The woman shook her head. "H-he had on a stock-ing c-cap."

"Did he leave a message for me?"

"A number...on—on the t-table."

For the first time, Taryn looked at him, her eyes completely unreadable, and he went to get the note while she comforted her mother-in-law.

He didn't recognize the handwriting, but the mes-sage was brief. They had until midnight to call. Of course, now that Nick knew the child was taken, it was unnecessary to wait. They'd want an exchange. Him for the girl.

"No, we don't want to call the police yet." Taryn stood, her gaze seeking his, while she pulled Olivia up. "Sit down," she said, when the woman looked as though she might collapse.

Olivia sank to a chair. Her startled gaze landed on Nick as though she was seeing him for the first time, and then she turned back to Taryn. "What are you saying? You have to call the police. They need—"

Taryn stooped to grasp the woman's shoulders and look her in the eyes. "You have to trust me, Olivia. Calling the police can get Lucy killed."

The older woman broke into hysterical sobs again, and he had to look away. What the hell had he done? Self-loathing ate a hole in his gut, blazed a fire in his veins. He was going to kill the bastard who'd done this.

The irony that he was equally responsible sliced through him like a cleaver.

"Let me see it." Taryn's voice was close, calm, in control, and he turned to find her holding out her hand.

He gave her the slip of paper and studied her drawn face as she scanned the words. Tension strained the corners of her mouth and the pulse at her neck beat wildly. But he was amazed at how composed she remained.

She looked up at him, her brows slightly furrowed as though she were deep in thought. Her mother-in-law let out a loud sob and Taryn glanced at the woman's bowed head, then motioned for him to follow her toward the kitchen.

As soon as they were out of earshot, she said, "Okay, this gives us a little over three hours."

He frowned, taken aback by what she was implying. "For what?"

"To get to them first." That look of concentration, of weighing and measuring, creased her face again. Obviously this was how Taryn handled a crisis. By emotionally detaching and focusing…methodically examining her options. She truly amazed him. Gave him hope. Maybe there was still a way out if they worked quickly, together….

She glanced over her shoulder at her mother-in-law, still crumpled in a heap. When Taryn faced him again, her expression was bleak. Her gaze met his, then flickered away.

But it was too late. He'd already seen it.

Her eyes were suspiciously bright.

He touched her arm, and she jumped a little. Her hand shot to her face. He intercepted it and used his thumb to dry the single tear that rolled down her cheek.

She looked at him, her eyes anguished and glassy. "Am I ever going to see her again?" she whispered.

Sharp, biting pain spiraled through Nick. He'd rather someone put a Magnum to his head than have to see the abject misery in her face. And he knew in this instant, there was nothing he wouldn't do to keep Taryn and her daughter safe.

Even if it meant giving up his own life.

He grabbed her upper arms and stared intently into her eyes. "Lucy will be all right. Do you hear me? I'm the one he wants. We're going to call right now and make the exchange."

She stared back, dazed-looking, her body swaying slightly. He wanted to pull her against him, wrap his arms around her and promise her the moon. But he'd lied to her enough.

She blinked a couple of times, jerked away and swiped at her face. "Will that guarantee Lucy's safety?"

Her voice was strong again, the wounded look

gone. The old Taryn was back, staring him down. Daring him to lie to her.

"No." He shook his head, his gaze steady with hers. "But it's our best shot."

"I don't agree." She glanced at the round wall clock over the ancient stove, pausing as her gaze snagged on the refrigerator door. Taped to it was a child's drawing with a big red heart around it. Taryn visibly swallowed and quickly looked away. "He doesn't know when we discovered Lucy missing. That's why he gave us until midnight. I say we use the time to hunt him down."

He frowned. "Bad idea."

"You think it's Maynard." She walked around him, past the oak kitchen table, picked up the yellow wall phone and started dialing. "We'll start with him."

"What are you doing?'

"Calling HPD."

He was ready to yank the receiver away from her when she held up her free hand to stop him. She didn't say a word, but he backed off and hoped to hell she knew what she was doing.

She identified herself and asked for a Detective Simon. Within seconds the guy was on the line, and after some purposeful flirting, Taryn asked him about Harrison's murder investigation.

The conversation only lasted a couple of minutes before she hung up. "The police don't have any leads. Cross and Maynard have been questioned. Sebastian hasn't been reached yet. He's on a plane due to arrive in London at any minute." She frowned. "Assuming he didn't get off in Dallas."

"What's that supposed to mean?"

"The pilot reported they were short one passenger after the Dallas stop. Come on." She didn't hang around to see his scowl, but headed toward her mother-in-law.

Agitated, Nick waited near the kitchen door while she comforted the older woman and gave her some instructions. He didn't believe Syd had anything to do with Harrison's murder. It just wasn't possible.

Dammit. Of course it was. Hell, Maynard and Syd could be in it together. The thought sickened him.

"Frankly, I don't want it to be Syd, either. But we can't rule him out," Taryn said, bringing him out of his self-absorbed preoccupation. "You have the keys?"

He inclined his head toward Olivia. "She going to be okay?"

"She'll get a friend to stay with her. She won't leave the house in case Lucy calls. But she won't contact the police."

"Wait a minute," he said as Taryn started to leave. She didn't question him when he ducked back into the kitchen and picked up the phone, only watched silently as he dialed Archie's number. He answered on the third ring, his voice already thick with sleep. Relieved, Nick lightly hung up the phone.

Renewed guilt made it hard to meet Taryn's gaze. Archie was home safe. Her daughter hadn't been so lucky.

She didn't ask, and he offered nothing as by tacit agreement they walked out. Taryn made sure the door was locked behind them, then they got in the rental car and headed for Dennis Maynard's apartment in the city.

Nick drove. She didn't argue. As admirably as

she'd pulled herself together, he could still see the tremor in her fingers, the quiver in her lower lip when she wasn't paying attention. He concentrated on the road, curbing his urge to speed, and let her have some privacy for a while. They had to talk soon, though. As much as he hated bringing up Archie, the fact that his friend hadn't been taken told Nick something.

"I'm glad Archie is safe," she said, her subdued voice pricking the silence. "You don't have to feel bad about it."

That she was so in tune with his thoughts unnerved the hell out of him. He'd never been an easy man to read. He liked it that way. "That means they don't know who I am for sure."

"I was thinking the same thing, or else Archie would have been the one they grabbed. Except I don't understand why anyone would think I'm the key, that I know where you…" She snorted. "Where Dylan Sands is." She paused, wariness and hope filling the brief lapse. "Could this be a bluff?"

He blew out a huff of air. "Sure wish I had a definitive answer. Although it is possible."

"Who's Priscilla Racine?"

He glanced over at Taryn, but it was dark and he couldn't see her face. "Why bring her up all of a sudden?"

"You didn't want me talking to her. I don't know…you seemed protective of her." She sounded defensive. "If she's someone you care about, I thought maybe you might want to make sure she's okay, too."

"They wouldn't bother with Priscilla. I stopped seeing her five months before I disappeared."

"By design? Or had the relationship fizzled out?"

Nick gripped the steering wheel a little tighter. Was her question personal or professional? He wasn't too crazy about how much satisfaction the personal angle would give him. "Both. We had only a casual thing going, physical mostly," he added, and saw Taryn stiffen slightly. "But I didn't want her to suffer any backlash over my disappearance."

"So you didn't want me questioning her and dragging up her name again."

"Exactly."

In the brief silence that followed, Nick pretty much guessed what she was thinking. He'd readily endangered Taryn but not Priscilla. The logic to that was absent, of course. He hadn't known Taryn when he hired her. Nor had he truly believed he was putting her at this great a risk. But he doubted that mattered in her present state of mind.

"Did you know she left a message on your answering machine a few months after you'd disappeared?"

"She's a flight attendant. When she was out of town, I'd be here, and vice versa. Sometimes we didn't see each other for a couple of months."

"But you said you'd stopped seeing her."

He shrugged. "I had, but I also said our relationship was mostly physical." Stupidly, he wanted Taryn to know there was nothing significant between him and Priscilla. Not that it mattered. After this was over, he had to disappear again. Out of Taryn's life. His chest tightened, and he cursed the crippling emotion that ambushed him.

Another silence stretched, which Nick used to second-guess their decision not to call the kidnapper right away. Taryn just kept looking at the digital clock.

Tracing the phone number would be useless, and in truth, going to Maynard's probably was, too. But he didn't know they suspected him and that was to their advantage. The pompous bastard would never expect to get caught. That might make him sloppy.

Nick muttered a curse. Talk about sloppy. He knew better than to be so single-minded. Cross and Syd weren't out of the picture yet. Although, Cross wasn't as viable a suspect. He didn't travel abroad that much. Which left Syd.

Taryn's gaze strayed toward Nick when she heard the foul word he'd mumbled, but she didn't ask what he was thinking. She welcomed the silence, the darkness inside the car, the inky blackness outside. It shrouded her senses, numbed the ugliness in her heart, disguised the shabbiness of her soul.

What kind of mother was she? Why hadn't she walked away from the business months ago? Other single parents made it, even if they had to work two and three jobs. What was with her obsession to provide some stupid dream life for Lucy?

Taryn herself had had the white lace canopy bed, the dollhouse in the backyard, private schools, endless music and dance lessons, and she'd turned her back on all of it. So why was it so important for her to give those things to Lucy?

Damn Derek. All their married life Taryn had scrupulously saved every cent she could hide from him in order to have the big house, the fine car and private school. And in one night it was gone, the husband, the money, the pretense of a marriage.

She swallowed back the guilt and shame. None of

that really mattered. The only thing her daughter had ever asked for was more time with her parents.

And now Taryn didn't know if she'd ever see Lucy again.

Blindly she felt for the window control. She needed air. Desperately. She pushed the switch and lowered the glass. Stifling humid air immediately slapped her face.

She gasped. The silence and darkness were no longer her ally. She should have kept talking to Nick, kept her mind occupied.

''What's wrong?'' he asked.

''Pull over.''

''Taryn?''

''Dammit. Pull over.''

He swerved the car off to the shoulder, and she opened the door and stumbled out. A few feet from the Ford Taurus, she bent over and emptied her stomach.

She'd barely had anything in her to begin with, but she was afraid to straighten, afraid she was going to be sick again. Dropping to a crouch, she flattened her palm on the ground to steady herself. Sharp, jagged gravel dug into her skin.

''Taryn?'' Nick lowered himself beside her.

The Taurus idled behind them. Several cars raced by on the freeway. There wasn't much light. She was grateful. ''I'll be okay. Just give me a minute.''

He laid a hand on her arm. She jerked away.

''We're stopping at the next pay phone.'' His voice was firm, unyielding. ''I'll talk to them. They'll make the exchange.''

''You keep saying 'they, them.' We don't even know who the hell we're dealing with. You can't be certain they'll give Lucy back.'' She heard herself speaking, knew the words were coming out of her mouth, but the rising panic in her chest made her voice sound shrill, savage. As though it belonged to someone else.

Nick stood and, against her will, pulled her up with him. ''Is that what you think?'' He held her by the arms, his grip almost painful. ''Is that what you want to believe?''

She broke away and swung at him, but he ducked out of the way. ''I hate you.''

''I know.'' He took one of her arms again and kept her from losing her footing.

A breath shuddered in her chest, and she slowly shook her head. A passing car provided enough light that she got a brief glimpse of the pain mirrored in his face. She opened her mouth to speak, but she couldn't.

He made an odd guttural noise, then hauled her roughly to him, wrapping his arms around her, imprisoning hers at her side. She sagged against his chest, too numb to struggle. Or even think.

''Ah, baby, I'll get her back.'' His heart thumped steadily against her breasts. His hands moved down her back, stroking, comforting. ''I promise you.''

A sad smile touched her lips. He wasn't capable of making that vow. But she knew he meant it. He'd turn himself over to save Lucy. Taryn wasn't so sure Derek would have done that for his own daughter.

She shifted, and he loosened his arms. She brought her hand up and, sighing, patted his chest before breaking away. ''Let's get moving. We don't have much time.''

He hesitated. ''I really think—''

"She's my daughter and I'm calling the shots."
She took a deep breath and prayed to God she knew
what she was doing. "Give me my cell phone battery
and I'll call Maynard's apartment. It sure as hell
doesn't matter if our calls are traced now."

She climbed into the car, and Nick was behind the
wheel in an instant. He didn't agree with her. That
was plain in the rigid set of his shoulders, the grim
line of his jaw. But he didn't argue, just tossed her
the battery, then pulled the car back onto the freeway.

In spite of everything that had happened, he was a
good man. She wanted to claw his eyes out right now,
but she did trust him. He'd had the opportunity to run
out on her, but he hadn't taken the weasel way out.

Nor had he led her on or tried to sweet-talk her.
His only promise was to get Lucy back. He wasn't
the type of guy to get emotionally involved. He'd
driven that fact home earlier when he spoke of Priscilla Racine. Their relationship had only been physical, he'd said more than once, and Taryn had gotten
the message.

Not that she wanted anything more from him. Not
that she could even think about anything but Lucy.

In fact, right now, Taryn wished like hell she'd
never laid eyes on Nick Travis.

Chapter Thirteen

Dennis Maynard lived in a fashionable town house in a swanky neighborhood off Memorial Drive. The place was dark, which didn't surprise Taryn since she'd gotten no answer when she'd called.

Nick drove them past the short driveway and parked the car half a block down the tree-lined street behind a Jeep. He cut the engine, his gaze darting around the landscape before he turned to look at her. "You should wait here."

"Yeah, right." Her laugh was a short bark of disbelief as she lifted the door handle.

"Think about it. If he does have Lucy, it's doubtful he has her here. I'm hoping we at least find a clue as to where she is. But you don't know Maynard. He's cagey, and if by some fluke he is here or comes home…"

He didn't have to finish. She knew what he was saying and it made sense. She shook her head. "I can't wait here. We'll split up when we get inside. That way we can cover more ground, and if he does show up we'll have a better chance of outmaneuvering him."

He sighed his frustration and got out of the car,

closing the door soundlessly behind him. She did the same, then followed him down the sidewalk, keeping a careful watch down both sides of the street.

It was late, and fortunately no neighbors were out for a stroll or walking their dogs. While she kept a lookout, Nick fiddled around the sides of the house. If necessary, she could break in through the front door, but light coming from both a street lamp and the adjoining town house made that prospect risky. Besides, the house probably had an alarm.

"Over here," Nick whispered.

Squinting into the semidarkness, she saw him near the garage and ducked through the shadows to join him.

"I've gotten this window open. It's small and the door to the house may be locked, but we'll have a better chance of not being seen breaking in from in the garage."

"I'll go first."

"Here." He linked his hands together to boost her up.

She wiggled through the narrow opening and wondered how he expected to make it through. Of course, his hips were slimmer than hers, but his shoulders were awfully broad.

With a few twists and a muffled grunt, he made it through and nearly landed on top of her. She scrambled out of the way and knocked over something metal. It hit the floor, the crash echoing off the walls.

She bit back a curse and remained perfectly still. Darkness engulfed her. Only two streams of murky light filtered through the wall seams and she couldn't see Nick's face. Another moment and her eyes adjusted enough that she could see his outline.

"You okay?" he whispered.

"Yeah," she said, surprised. Derek would have called her a stupid bitch, not ask if she was all right.

They waited in silence for a few minutes, then he said, "I think we're clear. Hopefully, the neighbors think it was a stray animal. But we're going to have to be careful about not turning on any lights."

"I do have this." She pulled a key chain flashlight out of her pocket and cupped the end with her other hand before she flicked it on. Aiming it at the floor, she slowly allowed the small circle of light to escape. It wasn't much but it helped.

"That's all we need." His hand awkwardly found hers. "Let's try the door."

"Wait. He probably has an alarm system."

"Not anymore." Something in Nick's voice chilled her, reminding her how little she knew him.

She swung the light ahead of them to make sure nothing was in the way. Several one-gallon paint drums and two bags of potting soil were stacked near the wall where they'd climbed in. A rake stood nearby and a broom leaned against the door frame, but that was it. The area was clear.

She pointed the way with the light but Nick went first, his grip of her hand unnecessary but comforting. He tried the doorknob and when it wouldn't budge, he pulled something out of his pocket and had the lock picked in seconds.

A night-light partially illuminated the short hall into the kitchen and living room. From there it wasn't quite so dark with a street lamp shining through the slanted miniblinds.

Both the decor and cleanliness of the place surprised Taryn. Like Nick's old apartment, the furnishings and artwork were expensive, tasteful. Which totally contradicted the boorish man she'd met. The place was clean and uncluttered, too, almost as though no one actually lived here.

She released Nick's hand and ran a finger across the top of an antique Chinese chest. No dust.

Watching her, he said, "I'm sure the agency arranged for this place, just like they did mine."

"It doesn't look like he even lives here. Are you sure this is his place?"

"I'm sure." His gaze swept the living room and the formal dining room with its massive marble table and white upholstered chairs. Everything was in its place. "Let's check out his bedroom. See if he has a den."

As soon as they entered the master bedroom Taryn saw evidence of Dennis Maynard. Several mismatched pairs of cowboy boots lay scattered across the snow-white carpet, and a pile of dirty clothes was heaped near the open closet. At least, she assumed they were dirty, judging by the faint but foul smell in the room.

"Yup, we're definitely in the right house," Nick muttered.

"Reassuring, isn't it?" Her sarcasm turned to disgust when she lifted a stack of papers with the toe of her shoe and found a plate of half eaten food crawling with roaches. "What a pig."

"That's our boy." Nick picked up a small reading lamp, set it on the floor in the corner and turned it on.

It provided just enough illumination to do some digging around yet not alert anyone outside. Taryn immediately headed for the bedside telephone. Beside it were a message pad and digital alarm clock. The bright red numbers made her stomach constrict. They were running out of time.

"Let's split up," she said, quickly scanning the scribbling on the pad—a dental appointment reminder for next Tuesday. Apparently he wasn't planning on leaving town soon.

"I'll go look for a den or study where he might keep papers. Taryn?"

She looked up.

His expression was grim. "Let's give ourselves fifteen minutes, then move on."

Her gaze automatically drew to the clock again, and she nodded and passed him the small flashlight. Before Nick even got to the door she started tearing through stacks of gun magazines and pornography. She kicked the pile of clothes to the side, saw there was nothing beneath it and kicked it back into a pile. One good thing about the place being such a mess was that he probably wouldn't know anyone had been here.

His walk-in closet wasn't in much better shape, and neither were his dresser drawers, but she was satisfied she'd done a fairly thorough job of rifling through everything by the time Nick reappeared.

"Anything?" she asked, but could tell by his bleak expression he'd come up empty.

He shook his head. "The guest room was neat and easy to check. The desk in his study was unlocked. But I couldn't find a damn thing."

She wasn't surprised. But disappointment and fear still squeezed her heart. She pushed them aside. Emotion would slow her down, cloud her reasoning. "Now Cross?" she asked.

"Syd's place is on the way."

"Okay." She stooped to shut off the reading lamp. Nick didn't want to believe Syd was involved, and she could hear in his voice how much this next stop would cost him.

Heaven help her, but since they'd found nothing here, now she hoped it was Syd.

Nick held on to the flashlight as they retraced their steps down the hall and through the living room. He stopped near the foyer. "Oh, hell."

"What?" She followed his gaze in the direction of the beam of light. A path of dirt marred the pristine white carpet.

"We must have tracked it in from the garage," he said. "But at this point, I guess it doesn't matter if he knows we've been here."

Taryn inhaled that same peculiar smell she'd noticed in his room. She could have sworn it wasn't out here before. Unnerved, she glanced around. Nothing looked out of place.

Nick touched her arm. "The front door."

She nodded her agreement. It didn't matter now and it would save time.

The ride to Syd's apartment was short and silent. When they pulled in front of the trendy uptown highrise, Taryn remembered something that had bothered her early on. It probably meant nothing right now, but she wasn't about to ignore any possibility.

"You had a long-term, prepaid lease on your apartment," she said as they entered the elevator. "I couldn't find a single lead on who'd paid all that money in advance."

Nick's smile was wry. "The agency. I think they

probably own the place, but have it arranged to look like I leased it. That's the only reason I can think of why they've left it vacant. They'd set me up there from the beginning, arranged for my identity and cover.''

"Identity? Cover?" She frowned, and then recognition dawned. "You're not even Dylan Sands?"

"Legally, now, yeah. Was I born with that name?" He shook his head. "Want to hear something really ironic? My given name is Nicholas.''

She was glad. Although she couldn't say why. Maybe because he seemed more like a Nick than a Dylan to her. "Wasn't that risky to take your old name back?"

"Nah, it was actually Nicholas James O'Roarke, after my father, but everyone called me Jim so they wouldn't confuse us. If I thought it was risky, I wouldn't have done it, but it felt good to reclaim something. Kind of like, up yours.''

Taryn smiled. That surprised her. She didn't think she'd ever be able to do that again. But as soon as they got off on the sixteenth floor her heart started to pound and her stomach got queasy.

She couldn't remember too many prayers she'd said as a child, but she pulled what she could out of her memory bank and made up the rest. A phone call had already told them no one was home, so as Nick stood guard, she picked the lock.

Syd's apartment wasn't quite as sterile. Mementos of his travels were scattered throughout the living room; African masks decorated the walls, primitive sculptures sat on a pair of marble pedestals. But like Maynard's, the place was in immaculate order. And if it wasn't for the half-full glass of milk on the end table, it would look as though no one lived here, either.

Taryn stared at the milk, her pulse quickening. Strange drink for a grown man. Not unheard of, but still...

"Syd is a bit of a health nut," Nick said, and she glanced over to see him staring at the milk, too. "He doesn't drink alcohol or sodas, so don't get your hopes up."

She rushed toward the short hall she presumed led to the bedrooms. There were only three doors. Behind the first one was a study—a desk, two chairs, a rowing machine. Nothing looked out of the ordinary. It could wait.

The door on the right was open and led to a bathroom. Spotless. Unused. Taking a deep breath, she turned to the last one. Nick was already there, his hand on the doorknob. Conflicting emotions darkened his eyes. He pushed the door open and flipped on the light.

It was a cavernous room, but her gaze automatically drew to the jungle-print quilt that covered the king-size bed. Perfectly made up. Not even a throw pillow out of place. The rest of the room was just as tidy. The only things the least bit out of place were a brown leather suitcase sitting on the floor near the closet, and a Macy's bag left on an overstuffed chair.

Nick entered the room first, ducking his head in for a look at the master bath, then walking toward the bed and dresser. Taryn had gotten to the walk-in closet when she heard the crinkling of the paper bag. Nick's savage curse.

She turned to find him holding a brand-new, still-packaged Barbie doll. Something that might entertain a ten-year-old girl.

Her entire nervous system short-circuited. Bile rose in her throat. Her heart pounded faster than a jackhammer. She moved toward him, her legs feeling like two-ton weights, and held out her hand.

"Let's not jump to conclusions. This could be a gift for his niece, or a friend's daughter." Not looking at all convinced, he passed her the doll and the bag.

"Does he have a niece?" she asked, her voice sounding amazingly calm.

"We didn't talk about our personal lives."

She pulled out the store receipt. The doll had been purchased just this morning. "Are you going to continue to defend him, or help me find my daughter?" she asked, looking up into his darkening face.

"What do you think?" he asked quietly, his eyes holding hers captive.

He hadn't run out on her. He was here, doing everything he could, and she should probably feel ashamed. But fear drove every other emotion from her being. "I'll go check the den. You finish in here."

"It's time to call, Taryn."

"No. We have another hour. We'll finish here, then go to Cross's place like we planned." She hesitated. "After that, we call." They both knew what that meant. She didn't have to spell it out. She would do anything to get her daughter back. God help her, even if it meant sacrificing Nick.

"Taryn, we don't have to wait—"

"Don't." She raised a hand to stop him. Enough guilt gnawed at her. "We stick to the plan."

Nick slowly nodded, then watched her leave the room. He couldn't imagine how hard this was for her, trying to bottle up her emotions and stay logical enough to search for clues. She was a tough lady. Smart, too. And beautiful. God, he wanted to hold her in his arms and promise everything would turn out okay. But they'd both know he'd be lying.

He didn't even know what the right thing was to do. In an hour they'd have no choice but to offer an exchange. Even if they didn't know who he was, he'd have to reveal his identity in order to get Lucy back. That might be the only way he could insure her safety.

In a perverse way he half wished it was Syd who was behind the kidnapping. Syd knew Nick. He knew Nick's word was good. And he knew Nick would honor any bargain they made for Lucy's safe return.

Still, it was difficult to reconcile Syd with the two unauthorized bombings in the Middle East last year where a dozen innocent civilians had died. Or the assassination of three American dissidents in China the year before. The list of heinous infractions was too long to contemplate.

Nick finished rifling through the night stands, then tackled the closet, checking each suit jacket and shirt pocket, hoping an overlooked slip of paper might lead them in the right direction. He had to forcibly put out of his mind the fact that these were Syd's clothes he was searching, the friend who'd played squash with him on Saturdays, the only guy in the agency besides Harrison with whom Nick had ever bonded. Or as close as Nick ever got to bonding with anyone.

That's why he had to distance himself emotionally. Like Taryn had. Already he had the feeling he'd missed something. Ever since they'd left Maynard's place, it had nagged at him, the sensation that some little inconsistency was staring him in the face. But he couldn't quite grasp it.

No one leaves the agency.

He mentally repeated the note they'd left for him. No question it was a warning, but vague enough to make him think they didn't know who he was. Besides, if they had known for sure, there would have been no forewarning. He'd already be dead.

"Do you know who Melissa is?"

Taryn's voice came from behind. He backed out of the closet. There was nothing in there. "I don't recall."

"Her name's on his day planner for Thursday. Apparently it's her birthday."

His gaze left Taryn's emotionless face and was drawn to the doll. He should feel something. Hope. Relief. He felt nothing. "Is that all you found in there?"

She nodded grimly.

"I wasn't any luckier. You ready to head for Cross's place?"

Again she nodded, then wordlessly turned around and led them down the hall.

When she told him she wanted to drive, he didn't argue. He simply climbed into the passenger side and ignored the fact that she paid little attention to the speed limit. His sudden preoccupation with the day's events consumed him.

Dammit. What was he missing?

"Want to let me in on what's bothering you?" At a red light, Taryn glanced over at him. "Is it about Syd?"

Shaking his head, he raked a hand through his hair.

"I'm trying to start from the beginning. What tipped them off? If I could figure that out…"

"You honestly don't think it was Harrison?" she asked softly.

"No. That's not emotion talking, either. He wanted to get those bastards possibly even more than I do. Besides, he wouldn't have given me up. It wasn't in his character."

Taryn didn't say anything for a long time and Nick knew what she was thinking. But she didn't know Harrison. Anyway, no one had any way of knowing that Harrison knew Nick was still alive. They'd been careful, rarely making contact and using pay phones when they did in case his office was bugged.

"I wouldn't have brought this up," she said finally, her voice hesitant, "but you probably ought to know, considering…" She paused and he heard her take a deep breath. "My police contact said Harrison was tortured rather thoroughly."

He briefly closed his eyes against the pain and guilt that sliced through him. This wasn't a surprise, and he'd already considered how torture could do odd things to a man's character, but hearing the words, knowing full well what they meant, brought on a fresh surge of grief and despair.

"I still don't think he cracked," he finally said when he could speak. "He'd been sick and in weak condition for quite a while. He probably didn't have to endure much before…"

When his voice broke off, she reached over and squeezed his hand. Her palm against his skin was warm and reassuring, and when she withdrew it he immediately felt the loss. Not that he deserved her kindness. Her contempt, yes. In fact, anything she wanted to dish out, he deserved. But that wasn't her style. She was truly a remarkable woman. He wished he'd met her sooner. But of course, his ties to the agency would have precluded him from having any kind of significant relationship.

He'd sold his soul the day two men in sharp-looking suits had come to him, lavishing him with praise and attention. Telling him how his knowledge and appreciation of the arts made him perfect for the job, how he had the sophistication and savvy to become a top agent. Everything he'd ever wanted to hear from his father, these two strangers had told him, and he'd soaked up the acclaim and approval like a thirsty sponge.

So young and gullible he'd been, he thought, staring out the window at the blur of headlights, with an ego the size of Manhattan. Yeah, he'd been perfect for the job, all right.

They were only a mile from Richard Cross's house, but traffic had picked up near the Richmond and Fountainview intersection and Taryn had to slow down. "If we're going to rule Harrison out, then what about Archie?"

Her question hit a nerve. Nick had already considered the possibility that Archie had figured out who he was and they'd gotten to him, but Nick had dismissed it as soon as he'd heard his friend's voice on the phone.

Again he forced himself to emotionally detach. "Archie didn't really know it was me."

"Yeah, but he recognized something about you that made him think you were Dylan's brother. That fits with your theory that they don't know for sure who you are. He could have told them you looked like Sands and that—''

"But he's okay," he said, cutting her off, unable to bear thinking he'd endangered the old man. "He answered the phone."

"They didn't necessarily have to hurt him to get information out of him."

He knew these people and what they were capable of. They used the most expedient measures, no matter how brutal. He shook his head. As painful as it was, he had no choice but to consider Archie as a possible source.

Arrogance. That was the root of Nick's problem. He'd had no business interacting with the man. It had been too risky, but Nick thought he was too smart, that he'd outwitted the agency. After all, he was wearing the white hat, wasn't he?

Taryn let out a pithy four-letter word and he looked up to find they'd missed the second green light in a row. "If we have to sit through another red light, I'm crossing the median and making a U-turn."

"We'll make the next one." He glanced over his shoulder at the car hemming them in. "Besides, it's too tight. You'll never get out of here."

"There's always a way out," she muttered, stretching to check the rearview mirror.

Nick grunted. Yeah, right. That's what he had thought. Look where he'd ended up.

No one leaves the agency.

The words from the message popped into his head again. Something nagged at him. Why the hell couldn't he come up with—

At his sharp intake of breath, Taryn turned to look at him. "What is it?"

"Remember the dirt we tracked into Maynard's town house? Do you recall any sort of peculiar odor to it?"

She shrugged. "There was something foul-smelling in his room...but I figured... I don't know. What are you getting at?"

The light turned green and someone behind them blared their horn. Muttering, she turned her attention back to the road and inched along behind the car in front of them.

Nick's heart raced and his palms started to sweat as bits of conversation and old scenes replayed in his head. He hoped he was wrong, but it suddenly all made sense. So damn much sense. God, he'd been a fool.

"Turn around," he said just as they entered the intersection.

She darted him a look. "What? Now?"

"I think I know where Lucy is."

Chapter Fourteen

It took only a few seconds for his words to register, and another for Taryn to see an opening in traffic and give the wheel a sharp turn. The tires screeched and angry horns blared. She almost hit the car coming from the opposite direction. The driver yelled and flipped her off.

But they were headed in the direction from which they'd come and she forced herself to breathe. "Where are we going? Where's Lucy?"

Nick exhaled a sound of relief. "I could be wrong, so—"

"Where, dammit?"

"My place."

Her foot automatically slackened on the accelerator and she stared at him. "Your old apartment?"

"Look out!"

She swerved just in time to avoid a head-on collision with a blue pickup. Her heart pounded so hard her leg got a little shaky and her foot couldn't keep the accelerator engaged. She let the car coast to the side for a moment to pull herself together.

"I'll take over." Nick started to get out of the car.

"No. I'm fine. I just need a second."

"Getting us killed isn't going to get Lucy back."

"Screw you, Travis."

"Go ahead, say it. Tell me what a jerk I am." His voice was calm, coaxing, almost. Maddening. "Get it all out."

"What? You want me to yell and scream so you can feel sorry for yourself and shed some guilt? Sorry, we don't have time for your tender feelings. Why do you think my daughter is at your old apartment?"

"This isn't about my feelings. You need a clear head. You have anything to say to me that's keeping you from concentrating, say it now."

She was too numb, too pumped full of adrenaline to think coherently. Although she probably should, she didn't even hate Nick. She just wanted to feel Lucy's soft blond hair against her cheek again. "I'm okay."

Her voice sounded weak and pitiful, and she despised herself for not having had the courage to get out of the business before now. If she held anyone accountable, it was herself. She'd been afraid to make a change, afraid she'd be a disappointment again.

"I'm listening," she said, and eased the car into traffic again.

"I assume you have a gun. Where is it?"

"One is in my car's glove compartment. The other is in my office."

"Damn. Why don't you carry it with you?"

"I don't usually." Most bounty hunters in Texas she knew didn't. It only made them more susceptible to accusations of kidnapping, or impersonating a police officer. "Besides, I didn't think this case required it," she added, sarcasm icing her tone.

Ignoring her, he picked up the cell phone she'd left

on the seat between them and punched in a number.
"Your office is closer. Let's swing by there and get
it."

Before he sent the call, he muttered an oath and
turned off the power.

"Who were you trying to call?"

"Archie. But that would be stupid. Another hang-
up call and they'd suspect something."

"Archie? Why—who do you think has Lucy?"
She could barely say her daughter's name without bile
rising in her throat, and she made a bargain with God
and herself. As soon as she got Lucy back she was
quitting. No more hanging around waiting for the big
score. No more time away from her daughter.

"The dirt we tracked into Maynard's town house,
it had a peculiar odor," he said, and she gave him a
skeptical look. "I know it was faint, but I recognized
it. It's prefertilized potting soil. Archie needs it for
his orchids. I used to pick it up for him."

She frowned. "Does Maynard know Archie?"

"No reason he should." His voice sounded
strained.

"So you think they got to him? But he answered
his phone and he sounded groggy, like he'd been
asleep." She shook her head, trying to make sense of
what Nick was saying. And then it hit her. Excitement
and hope churned in her belly. "You think they're
holding both Archie and Lucy at his apartment."

"Possibly."

Frustration exploded in her chest. "Possibly? What
the hell *are* you saying?"

"Archie might be involved. Maynard's taken my
place as his flunky."

He'd said it so quietly she thought she heard

wrong. They pulled up in front of her office and she cut the engine. "What did you say?"

"Go get the gun. We'll talk on the way."

In the interest of time, she obliged him. He got out of the car the same time she did, but he didn't go inside with her. He stayed near the door, glancing both ways down the street. It only took her a minute, and as soon as she stepped outside, he headed for the car and climbed in behind the wheel.

She didn't care for that move. It implied she wasn't going to like what he had to tell her. But she handed him the keys and got in beside him, her heart in her throat.

"I think Archie is involved in some way," he said without preamble. "I know it sounds crazy, but a lot of the puzzle pieces fit."

"As in, involved with Maynard and the agency?"

He nodded, his expression grim.

"You're right. It sounds crazy." She stared at him, wondering how worried she should be. He looked rational enough. "You'd better explain some more."

"No one leaves the agency," he murmured.

She waited for him to say something else, but he just stared ahead at the road, frowning, deep in thought "You're scaring me, Nick."

"What?" He blinked, and seemed to snap out of his meditative trance. "When an agent is too old, or sick, to be of use, where would he go?" He looked briefly at her but didn't wait for an answer. "He knows too much so they can't just cut him loose. Whenever anyone would start getting sentimental on Harrison, he'd joke about how the cancer was his ticket out of the agency. That he'd never get out any other way."

"Okay," she said slowly, trying to follow his thinking but failing. "But you already knew that. That's why you staged your disappearance."

"Yeah, but what if I stayed until I was no longer of value to them? What if Harrison had outlived the cancer and wanted to retire?"

A shiver ran down her spine. What he was implying was so cold-blooded. "You can't be serious. You think they would just—eliminate anyone who wasn't productive?"

"Or who could point a finger, or write a tell-all book."

"That's hard to believe."

"Not if you knew the agency's purpose, the things we've done in the name of our country."

"So what about Archie? He's still alive."

"He's still productive."

"Watching the Houston office—through you."

"You got it."

Taryn stared at the hard line of his profile, heard the trace of bitterness in his voice. She'd seen several sides to Nick firsthand, how he could be kind and compassionate and loyal. She'd learned a lot about him as Dylan Sands, too. Not all good, yet there was basic goodness in the man. But there was still that dark, dangerous dimension she'd probably never know. Didn't want to know.

"Okay," she said. "Sounds like you're convinced Archie is with the agency."

He looked at her then, briefly. Long enough for her to see the conflict of emotions plaguing him. "Sounds far-fetched, doesn't it?"

"You know the man. You tell me."

"That's the hard part. I don't want to believe it.

I've known the guy for over ten years. I met him the day the agency moved me into the apartment.'' He slid her a meaningful look. "Coincidence? Maybe. But an awful lot of things are starting to add up.'' He cursed and muttered, "Maybe I'm just going crazy.''

He paused when they stopped at the intersection before his apartment building and looked up toward the sky. "Archie's light is on.''

She followed his line of vision. The building was mostly dark except for a few lit units closer to the ground floor.

"Over there. On the far right. You can see a reflection off his greenhouse windows. There's a glow coming from behind. That's his living room. Normally he'd be asleep by now.''

Taryn squinted. She knew what he was talking about, but it was pretty flimsy evidence. As much as she wanted to believe she was close to getting Lucy, she thought Nick was off base in his theory. She'd seen stress and fear do stranger things to a man.

But why point the finger at Archie? The man had been a father figure to Nick. Denial alone would prevent him from believing his friend was capable of such betrayal. Was the thought of the old guy being taken that painful to Nick?

She laid a hand on his arm. "Maybe we should make that call now.''

"What time is it?'' he asked, without looking away from the apartment.

"Twenty to twelve.''

The light turned green and he steered the car through the intersection, then pulled off to the side half a block from the building's entrance.

"We still have time.'' He frowned. "Archie

wouldn't use his phone. That means one of them will have to leave to take the call at the number they left.'' He made a sound of disgust. ''Hell, Maynard probably has something rigged up. Some kind of call-forwarding. They have no way of knowing when you'd call. Besides, that would be just like him. One more way he can prove he's smarter.''

''Nick?''

''I say we don't wait. We can—''

''Nick!'' she said sternly, squeezing his arm, and he looked at her as if she was the crazy one. ''Do you know how...'' She sighed. ''How peculiar this all sounds? I mean, I want Lucy to be in there, too. I want this to be all over, but...''

He stared at her without speaking for a moment, and then his face relaxed and he breathed deeply. ''Believe me, I do know how this sounds. And I hate the thought that a friend I had trusted for ten years isn't who I thought he was.''

He paused, and she started to remind him that he'd been under a lot of stress, that no one would blame him for grasping at straws, but he put two fingers to her lips before she could get anything out of her mouth.

''Taryn, I know what I'm talking about. There've been a lot of inconsistencies in my relationship with Archie that I've been mulling over. I can't go into it all right now. Time is too short.'' His hand slid behind her neck until his palm cupped her nape. ''Please trust me. I'll get Lucy back.''

She swallowed. He looked so damn sincere.

''The worst that can happen is that we'll wake up Archie.''

He pulled her toward him and she didn't resist. She

closed her eyes and leaned her forehead against his. They both knew that wasn't the worst thing at all. "Okay," she whispered.

They let a few moments of steadying silence pass and then he asked, "Ready?"

"Ready."

They broke apart, and he picked up the gun. "You take this."

"What about you?"

"Hopefully neither one of us will need it."

"What are we going to do? You can't just knock on his door."

He got out of the car and she scrambled after him. "I can if I play dumb," he said, stepping into the shadows. "Neither Archie nor Maynard know we're on to them. And they aren't expecting us to show up here."

"So what are you going to do? Walk in and ask if you can search the apartment?"

"There's no way we're going to break in. Not with him being on the top floor like he is. The only way I'm going to get in is if I'm invited."

"You mean, we."

He stopped and grabbed her forearms, forcing her to face him. "You have to stay out of sight."

"She's my daughter, dammit."

"And if something goes wrong, who's going to save her?"

Taryn blinked. Her chest was tight, her breathing irregular. Damn him for being right. "What are you going to tell Archie?"

His grip turned into a caress as he stroked his hand up and down her arm. "That I *am* Dylan Sands's brother and I need to talk to him." One side of his mouth lifted slightly. "That should keep them at least a little off balance."

"What if he doesn't believe you? What if he knows who you are already?"

"Then he'll have what he wants," he said quietly. "And he won't have any reason to keep Lucy."

It was hard to look him in the eyes, knowing he was about to offer his head on a platter in exchange for her daughter. But when Taryn tried to duck her head, he hooked a finger under her chin and drew her gaze back to his.

"It's going to be all right," he whispered.

"You can't promise me that."

He blinked, and his hand fell from her chin. "No," he agreed. "No, I can't."

"Tell me one thing." Her heart started to pound again and she cursed herself for being so stupid. There was no point to this question. It would only upset her. "And I want the truth," she said, holding his gaze, daring him to lie. "Will they let her go?"

His expression didn't waver. "I don't know."

She exhaled slowly. She'd wanted the truth, she reminded herself, trying to tamp down the anger, the panic, that made her blood roar like wildfire through her veins. But if he'd lied, she could have savored hope a little longer. Damn him.

"You wanted the truth," he said softly.

She jerked away from him. "Let's go."

"Keep your cool, Taryn," he warned in a low voice as he easily kept pace with her. "You're going to need it."

He was right, of course, but she didn't respond. Not verbally. But she did concentrate on taking deep, calming breaths for the rest of the short walk to the building.

''Let's go up by way of the parking garage elevator,'' Nick said when she started for the entrance. ''We aren't as likely to run into anyone.''

She nodded at the grim reminder that this undertaking could have an unpredictable outcome. A violent one. She took another deep breath, then followed him through the underground structure, staying low, weaving in and out of cars until they got to the elevator.

She wondered if he'd noticed that Maynard's green sports car was nowhere in sight, which in itself didn't prove anything, and she decided not to mention it. Nick seemed convinced he was right about Archie and Maynard.

For her sake, she hoped he was right. But if he was, she couldn't imagine what kind of blow that was going to be to Nick. Once the adrenaline dried up and the excitement died, and everyone was safe, he was going to have some serious issues to deal with. He'd have more than his friend Harrison to grieve for, he'd mourn the loss of a relationship with a man that never really existed.

Betrayal was a hard pill to swallow. The aftermath of second-guessing and self-loathing for being such a fool would dig away at his confidence, at his ability to trust, until he was only a shell of a human being.

She understood all too well. Derek's lies and death had done that to her. Made her jaded. Hardened her heart. Sucked all the emotion out of her.

Except oddly, she'd trusted Nick. She still did.

His loyalty both irritated and impressed her. After all he'd been through, the ugliness he'd seen in his job, he still had more humanity and honor left in him than most people she knew. He'd defended Syd when it would have been easy to indict him, and he'd risked his life for Harrison. For principle.

And now he was risking his life for her daughter.

She thought again about how he could have run, and how she would never have known what the hell had happened. But he hadn't. He was here, taking responsibility. That said something.

"We'll get off on the eighteenth floor, then walk up the other three," he said as the elevator doors closed. "You stay on the landing until after I get inside the apartment."

She adjusted the fit of the gun tucked inside her waistband, frustration beginning to well up inside her. "Then what? How am I supposed to know what's going on in there?"

"I'll try to leave the door unlocked. But don't come inside unless you hear—" He gave her a wry smile. "You'll know when."

She didn't like it. Together they had a better chance. But he was right about Lucy. "What are you going to say?"

"Other than I'm Sands's brother?" He shrugged. "That I think he's not really dead and that something strange is going on." The doors slid open and he glanced down the hall before he led them to the stairs.

"You wouldn't show up at midnight to tell him that," she said once they started the climb.

He didn't bother to answer and she knew why. He didn't think he'd need an explanation. It was all going to be over in the next few minutes.

She gripped the handrail tighter, not sure her legs would hold her. This didn't feel right. Everything had happened too fast. Exactly the way she didn't operate. She liked to go slow, analyze, plan, know her adversary. Right now, her instincts were so skewed, she doubted she could remember how to tie her shoelaces.

It was no wonder. The two people she cared about the most were at risk.

At the sudden realization, her knees threatened to buckle again.

"Wait," she said when they got to the next landing.

Nick immediately turned and reached his hand out to her, concern in his eyes. "What's wrong?"

Her voice had come out shaky. She grasped his hand. "This is stupid. You're going in half cocked. I say we go ahead and make the call. They don't know where we are. We won't lose the element of surprise."

He came back down a step so that he could slip an arm around her. His expression was so tender when he smiled, she thought she was going to lose it. "What happened to trusting me?"

"This isn't about trust." A sudden shiver shot down her spine. Why was it so cold all of a sudden? "I want to do what's smart."

He pressed his lips together and said nothing at first. Then he stepped back up, releasing her. "Maybe you should wait in the car."

"Are you crazy?"

"You're too emotional."

"Of course I'm emotional. We're talking about my daughter."

"Exactly."

She returned his unwavering stare. "And you. We're talking about you."

He blinked. "Come on. We're wasting time." He turned without another word and took the stairs two at a time.

Screw him. She had a right to be worried about him, too. It wasn't as if she was asking for anything in return. Hurt and confused, she watched him disappear around the next curve, then hurried to catch up.

When they got to the twenty-first floor, Nick paused at the door to the corridor and checked his watch. He exhaled as he looked up. "Okay, wish me luck."

Their eyes met. She didn't know if she could do it. Stand here and wait. Do nothing. She felt the gun at her waist, which drew Nick's gaze. "You should take this."

He shook his head. "We stick to the plan." When she said nothing, he added, "Right?"

She nodded halfheartedly. "Be careful."

His lips curving slightly, he brought his hand up to brush her cheek. "You, too."

Again she nodded, unable to speak around the lump in her throat. And then she watched him silently disappear behind the door. Before it closed all the way, she stopped it with the toe of her sneakers and left a scant crack. Just enough so she could hear.

But after the knock on Archie's door, the only sound that reached her was muffled and unintelligible. In fact, the only voice she could hear at all was Nick's deep baritone. Then she heard the distinct click of the door closing. Or locking.

She muttered a curse, slowly opened the stairwell door wider and slipped into the corridor. Nick had better have somehow left Archie's door unlocked, she thought as she approached the apartment, staying to the side of the door, away from the peephole.

After listening for any sounds inside and hearing nothing, she turned the doorknob a fraction of an inch. And then another. She held her breath when the final turn disengaged the latch, then she slowly pushed the door in. With it partially open she could hear men's voices now, but nothing discernible. They were too distant. Probably coming from the living room off to the right. From what she remembered of the apartment layout, distant enough that she felt relatively confident pushing the door open wider.

Adrenaline fueling her, she edged inside. The foyer was clear and she slipped into the coat closet. She just about got the door closed, when out of the sliver left open, she saw Lucy sitting in the far corner bedroom.

Looking small and terrified.

Chapter Fifteen

Nick cast an inconspicuous glance around the apartment as Archie ushered him into the living room. He would have liked to have gotten a look into the second bedroom, which had been converted into a den some time ago, but Archie had led him in the opposite direction. Which in itself was odd. As was the fact that Archie was still fully dressed even though he'd sounded as though he'd been asleep when Nick had called earlier.

"This really is quite a surprise, Mr. Travis," the older man said over his shoulder. "A very pleasant one."

Nick smirked. This wasn't a surprise. He knew Archie too well. Or so he thought he had, Nick reflected wryly. "I'm sorry about the late hour, but I did have something rather urgent to discuss with you."

Archie lowered himself to his favorite blue-plaid recliner and leaned his cane against the arm. For a man to whom Nick was supposed to be a stranger, Archie didn't seem especially put out or even very curious. And then he frowned. "Oh, my, where are my manners? Would you like a cup of tea, Mr. Travis?"

"No, please." Nick held up a hand when Archie started to rise. "I won't be long." He paused and stayed standing when the other man motioned him to sit. "I think you know I'm not really Travis." He paused again and gauged Archie's remarkably blank expression. "And that I'm not Taryn Scott's brother."

His expression wavered slightly then, and an almost shrewd gleam entered his eyes. The sight made Nick a little ill, and he realized he'd still harbored the slimmest of hopes that he'd been wrong about his suspicions.

"Well…" Archie drawled, "I did think I saw a resemblance to Dylan, but I am an old man—"

"You were right," Nick cut in. "I'm Dylan's brother."

A sudden look of uncertainty raised the man's white brows. If Archie was a higher-up in the agency, he probably knew Nick had three brothers. Maybe Nick could bluff his way through this. "Really? Why tell me now?"

"Because he'd always spoken so fondly of you and—" Shrugging, Nick paced to the window. "I think he's in trouble."

After a thundering silence, Archie asked, "So you believe he's still alive?"

"Don't you?" Nick turned back to find Archie staring at him with such a calculating coldness that it made Nick's gut churn. How could he have so badly misjudged him? Had he been that desperate for a friend, for a father? But Nick no longer had any illusions or doubts now.

And from the sickeningly triumphant expression forming on Archie's face, he knew it.

"You disappointed me, Dylan," Archie said, shaking his head. He reached between the chair cushion and arm, and produced a 9 mm. "You really did. You know we'd have known if you had any contact with your former family. None of them could have tracked you down."

He thought briefly about denying who he was, maybe trying another bluff and stalling for a few more minutes, but the irony was too damn much. "I disappointed you?" He laughed, a humorless sound that didn't seem to faze Archie. "That's rich, Hanes. Ten years. For ten stinking years you played me. And I fell for it. Every minute."

He stared back, unblinking, his eyes cold. Like a robot, devoid of emotion. "You could have gone far, Dylan. So much potential. You threw it all away."

"Why kill Harrison, Archie? He only had six months left."

He narrowed his eyes, his gaze slightly unfocused as if his thoughts had strayed. "You were my choice to replace him. Did you know that?" He sighed. "Of course you didn't. But it became obvious a few years ago you weren't made of the right stuff. Far too honorable and impressed with the red, white and blue. But I liked you, Dylan, and I chose to ignore it. I'd hoped you'd come around. I haven't been wrong much in my career. You did disappoint me."

"Why kill Harrison?" Nick repeated, his anger growing, the blood pounding in his head.

Archie shrugged a shoulder. "He'd outlived his usefulness. We figured he knew where you were, but he refused to cooperate." His icy gaze purposefully connected with Nick's, and then a depraved smile curved his bloodless lips. "He turned out more useful dead. The, uh, unfortunate incident seems to have flushed you out.''

The urge to do violence to the man he once called his friend was so great, Nick had to clench his fists and steel them at his side. It didn't matter that the gun was aimed at his heart. He would have rushed the bastard and damn the consequences had it not been for the main reason he was here.

''Where is she?'' he asked, and when Archie lifted a brow in feigned ignorance, Nick growled, ''I want the girl released. Now.''

''See, Dylan…'' Shaking his head, Archie let out a sound of disgust. ''That's been your problem. You're too goddamn noble. Right and wrong is not as black and white as you think. You take this business in the Middle East—''

''Where is she?'' Nick advanced a step.

Archie cocked his head in amusement and fingered the trigger. Nick froze. ''As I was saying…you take this Middle East mess. Those people have no interest in negotiating or in establishing peace. They're nothing but vile terrorists, and as a nation we treat them like diplomats, call them leaders. When did we get to be such wimps, Dylan? We're supposed to be a world leader, goddamn it. Instead we sit here with our tail between our legs. Makes me sick to my stomach.''

Nick's own gut felt unsettled. Had he known this man at all, he wondered as he peered into his empty pale gray eyes. Although this time Nick wasn't fooled. They weren't as vacant as they seemed. Evil lurked there. Madness. ''So you've made yourself judge and jury, deciding who has the right to live and die.''

Archie looked at him as if he were the one who

was insane. "You still don't see the big picture. We're talking about a few men who control millions of people, about whom they don't really care. It's the power that motivates them. We just level the playing field. That's all."

"We? I assume you mean Maynard."

He nodded. "And a couple of others from New York who you don't know. The world's a big place, Dylan."

"Does Maynard have the girl?"

Archie smiled. "Your soft spot is showing again."

Nick summoned all the composure in his reserve. "I understand it was your job to watch me, and that it was nothing more than an assignment for you, but we did have some good times, Archie. We shared some laughs, and we—"

"You're wrong," he cut in angrily. "It wasn't just an assignment for me." For an instant, something that looked like regret softened his features. "At first it was, I admit, and I resented it a great deal. I wasn't ready to retire from the field, to be stuck in this apartment, shelved away like unwanted baggage. But I became genuinely fond of you, Dylan. That's why you disappointed me so much. I wanted you for my right-hand man. Not Maynard."

Nick glanced furtively at his watch. Taryn had to be crazed by now. He hadn't meant for Archie to go on like this. He'd only wanted to appeal to any sense of decency the man possibly still possessed, in hopes of getting Lucy released.

"I know you, Archie. At least well enough to know that you don't want that child hurt. For the sake of the good times we had, let her go." Nick watched the emotions play out across the older man's face. He seemed to be weakening a little as he stared off beyond Nick and the memories from the past ten years compelled him.

When several endless minutes of silence elapsed, Nick glanced at his watch again. If he had a chance of freeing Lucy, it was with Archie. Before Maynard showed up.

"Is she here, Archie?" Nick asked softly. "Do you have Lucy?"

He blinked, his eyes focusing more intently on Nick again. "The girl is fine." He looked old all of a sudden. Older than the seventy-three years he claimed to be, assuming that was the truth. "Did I tell you why I was assigned to you?" he asked. "I wasn't the only one who wanted you to replace Harrison. The higher-ups had you pegged for a leader from the beginning. They wanted you to head the agency here in Houston. I was supposed to confirm that you were the right guy. A real agency man." A look of disgust distorted his face. "It's ironic, really, that you probably did turn out to be the best candidate. The agency has gotten so screwed up. Soft. Just like you. Involved more in goddamn research than in putting things to rights.

"I really had no choice but to step in. I was tired of the United States being a damn doormat. Too many misdeeds were going unpunished. All in the name of diplomacy. With my connections and access to funding, it would have been downright unpatriotic of me not to do anything about it."

Nick ignored the churning in his belly and forced himself to smile. "Sure, I can understand that."

"No, you can't." Archie glared accusingly at him. "You're just like the rest of them. You disappointed me, Dylan. More than I can tell you. You should have been the one beside me.''

"I'm here now. No need to keep the girl. Tell me where she is and I'll send her—''

"Come on, Sands. You know damn well we can't do that." Maynard's voice came from behind, chilling Nick to the bone. "Remember, you're not the golden boy anymore. Nobody gives a damn what you want."

He turned to meet Maynard's contemptuous green eyes. Like Archie, he held a 9 mm. Except he had his aimed at Nick's face.

"So, Dennis, I see you elevated yourself to kidnapping helpless children."

"New face, same arrogant bastard." Squinting, Maynard stepped closer. "Vast improvement on the nose and chin. Too bad I'm going to obliterate them."

"Ah, they finally trained your species to use words with more than two syllables. Impressive."

"Shut up, Sands."

"Boys." Archie picked up his cane and leaning heavily on it, pushed to his feet. He relaxed the hand holding the gun, but it didn't matter since Maynard still had Nick covered. "Stop this nonsense. We have a long night ahead of us."

Frowning, Nick glanced at Maynard. Apparently, Archie's assertion surprised him, too. "I don't know what you have in mind," Nick said, "but I'm not saying or doing anything more until you let the girl go."

Maynard shrugged, an odious smile curving his mouth. "I don't care what you have to say." He pulled the trigger back a fraction. "I'll just pop you now."

Archie banged his cane against the table. At the

loud noise, Maynard jerked. Nick braced himself for a bullet.

Nothing.

"Enough, Dennis." Archie moved around the coffee table to stand closer to Nick. "Who else knows about us?"

The presumption that the investigation went beyond him and Harrison surprised Nick. Gave him hope. Possibly ammunition...

"Besides Taryn, of course," Archie said.

Nick snapped out of his preoccupation. "She doesn't know anything."

The older man gave him a patronizing smile. "Come on, Dylan."

"Why would I have told her anything? I knew you for ten years. I trusted you," he added, and was gratified to see a flicker of remorse in the man's eyes. "Yet I never once betrayed my position with the agency. As far as you were concerned, I was an importer."

"True enough." Archie pursed his lips. "But then again—"

"You weren't banging him," Maynard cut in, smirking.

Nick's control started to slip, but as he turned toward the scumbag, he forced himself to think of Taryn. Of Lucy. "Taryn Scott knows nothing. She thinks I'm a lawyer trying to deliver an inheritance to Dylan Sands."

"Yeah?" Maynard laughed, the wicked sound scraping Nick raw. "And who does she think we are? Friendly neighborhood child-care providers?"

"Obviously she knows there's more to the story than I'd given her, but that's it," Nick said calmly.

"She doesn't even know where I am right now. The only thing she knows for sure is that she wants her daughter back. Deliver, and you won't hear from Taryn Scott again."

"I wish we could believe that," Archie said. "I truly do. I didn't even want to take the child."

"Why did you? Obviously you knew who I was. Why not just grab me?"

"I wasn't sure it was you. I only knew you weren't the young lady's brother." The man's smile was wry. "Not the way you looked at her."

Nick mentally shook his head at the irony. It hadn't been his mannerisms or even his arrogance that had given him away. His stupidity had. For more than a decade he'd kept his feelings under wraps, carefully kept his distance from emotional entanglements. From his family. Women he dated. Even with Archie to some degree.

But he'd screwed up with Taryn. The one person for whom he'd gladly lay down his life, give up everything that he cared about. And now his stupidity could cost her the only person she held dear. What a worthless, self-absorbed ass he'd been.

"That's why we took the child," Archie said, and motioned with his eyes and a tilt of his head to Maynard. "If it *was* you, I knew you'd reveal yourself. You wouldn't let her die."

The knife of guilt dug deeper. But relief comforted him, too, when Maynard left the room. To get Lucy, Nick prayed. "And here I am. Let her go, Archie."

"I wish we could. You do know me, Dylan," he said with such genuine regret that Nick nearly wanted to believe him. "I don't like this messy business of involving children. I really, really don't." He shook his head, looking extremely agitated. Unstable, almost. And then his eyes lit up at something behind Nick. "Here she is."

Nick turned around, and his gut constricted painfully. A tiny version of Taryn with the same long blond hair and blue eyes stood beside Maynard. Except her eyes were wide with fright and her cheeks blotchy from crying. The nauseating image of the man's hand resting on her slim shoulder made Nick want to vomit.

Breathing out slowly, he said, "Hi, Lucy. I'm a friend of your mom's."

She said nothing, only stared back at him with distrust and fear clouding her pale face.

He turned back to Archie. "Have Maynard take her down to the lobby and let me make a call to her mother. You can listen in. This can all be over soon without any innocent bystanders getting hurt."

Archie sighed. "You weren't listening. I tried to tell you how much I hate this business of involving a child. But it's too late. She's seen and heard too much. If only she'd been a little younger..."

Nick stared in stunned disbelief. "You stupid crazy old bastard—"

Maynard started laughing, and out of the corner of Nick's eye, he saw him raise his gun.

A loud shriek came from behind them.

Taryn lunged forward, kicking the gun out of Maynard's hand. She grabbed Lucy and pulled her to the side just as Archie leveled his gun at them.

Nick rushed Archie, manacling his wrist and sabotaging his aim. But the gun went off, once, twice, before he could shake the weapon free from Archie's grasp.

With a sinking feeling, Nick spun toward Taryn.

Several feet away from her, Maynard clutched his stomach, blood oozing from beneath his hand. He stared at the wound for a long silent moment before lifting his stunned gaze to Nick.

Then he fell into a lifeless heap on the crimson-splattered white carpet.

Taryn hugged Lucy to her, nestling her face against her breasts and sparing the sobbing child the horror of Maynard's bloody death.

Nick turned back to Archie with the sudden realization that the old man had quit struggling. His wrist dangled limply in Nick's hand, and the gun lay on the carpet at his feet. His free hand was splayed across his chest. Just over his heart. His skin had turned a sickly gray.

Nick kicked the gun away, then released him. The old man slumped to the floor, gasping for air, clutching in desperation at his heart. In spite of himself, a twinge of sympathy mixed with regret pricked Nick.

He looked away and met Taryn's eyes. Still holding Lucy and stroking her shuddering back, Taryn had moved them farther away, at the edge of the foyer from where she watched Nick with a wariness he couldn't interpret.

There was so much to say to her. More apologies to make. Now wasn't the time. He hoped to have another opportunity. He doubted he would. "We have to move." He forced his attention away from the painful image of her soothing her terrified child, and back to the gory scene at his feet. "Before the police get here."

"Why? We're in the clear. I know half the department. I can explain—"

"I can't be here, Taryn. Neither can Dylan Sands."

She blinked and visibly swallowed. "It's not over for you, is it?"

"Essentially."

"But Harrison was the only one who could really clear you. Explain why you disappeared. That you had nothing to do with—" Understanding clouded her expression, and her voice had gone flat with defeat, maybe even disappointment.

Or maybe that's what he wanted to believe. That she wanted him to stay. Even though it was impossible.

Her gaze strayed to Archie. He was still alive. Barely. "We should call an ambulance."

"Get Lucy out. Go ahead. Take the car."

"What about you?"

Sirens blared in the distance. Nick grimaced. Taryn stiffened. Of course someone had called the police in response to the gunshots. "You still have your gun?" he asked.

"Yes."

"Touch anything besides doorknobs, the usual?" He yanked a linen towel off a rack behind the wet bar and quickly began wiping the furniture, the gun he'd grabbed from Archie.

She shook her head.

The sirens got closer. "Go, Taryn."

"Fingerprints won't matter. I've been investigating Sands. I had a reason to be here. They'll eventually question me, anyway."

"Taryn. Now."

"Come with us."

Their gazes locked for a moment. He was so damn tempted. A small fire would take care of most of the evidence and yet be easily extinguished. Still, too risky. The building was heavily populated.

His gaze drifted to Lucy. She looked small for ten, but Nick knew little about kids. Wrapped in her mother's arms, her face hidden, at least she had calmed down. But God only knew how traumatized she'd been. All because of him.

"Take the elevator to the parking garage. The lobby's probably crawling with people already." He strode past them, opened the door and checked the empty corridor. "It's clear."

Taryn hesitated, her gaze probing, confused, and then she carefully kept Lucy's face turned away from the carnage in the living room while she guided the child toward the open door.

"I'll catch up with you later," he said, then averted his cowardly eyes.

Even though she already knew he was lying.

Chapter Sixteen

•

Taryn picked up her mug of tea, knowing it had long ago grown cold. She didn't care. She sipped, then stretched out the kink that four straight hours sitting in her lumpy office chair had given her, and continued to watch her sleeping daughter. It was a miraculous and deeply satisfying sight, visible assurance that she was unharmed and safe here on the ugly brown couch Taryn and Derek had bought for the office out of their first recovery check.

Lucy's blond lashes fluttered against her satiny cheeks, and unable to resist, Taryn leaned forward to brush the bangs off her daughter's forehead. Sleepy blue eyes slowly opened. They widened suddenly, a flash of fear darkening them, sending an arrow of guilt to Taryn's heart. But recognition just as quickly dawned, and a grin curved her mouth. And then she yawned.

"Hi, sleepyhead." Taryn touched her soft cheek.

"I almost forgot we were in your office," Lucy said, her gaze roaming the bare peeling walls. "I haven't been here since I was a kid."

Taryn smiled. She had purposely kept Lucy away from the seediness of the business. But last night somehow, this seemed like the best place to run to. She couldn't explain why, maybe because it was the closest, or so ironically familiar to Taryn, or perhaps because it was the least likely place the police would look to question her in the early morning hours. She didn't really know.

It didn't matter, she thought as she peered contentedly into her daughter's face. Lucy was safe. "Hungry?" she asked.

Lucy wrinkled her nose in thought, then her gaze wandered over to the battered oak desk by the window and a grin tugged at her mouth. "Like for a candy bar?"

Taryn chuckled, shaking her head. Amazing how the kid could remember where Taryn kept her stash, yet she couldn't seem to recall when or if she'd done her homework most weekends. "Oh, I suppose I could scare up a bag of peanut M&M's. But I sort of had a real breakfast in mind."

"I'll take the M&M's," Lucy said, her expression suddenly serious. "Did you call Gramms? I don't want her to worry about us."

Taryn nodded, emotion coiling into a lump in her throat. Her daughter was growing up so fast. "As soon as you fell asleep. She knows we're here and that you're safe."

"That man scared her," Lucy whispered.

Taryn swallowed. "I know, honey, and I'm so sorry that happened to you and Gramms." She got up to sit next to Lucy on the edge of the couch. Her hand felt so small and fragile in Taryn's. "But it will never happen again. Ever. I promise."

Lucy smiled tentatively. "Are you really going to quit your job and live with me all the time?"

"You bet I am. Starting today."

"Today?" Lucy's eyes widened. "Really?"

"Really."

"But what about—"

"No buts," Taryn cut in. She knew what her daughter was going to say because they'd had prior similar conversations. But this time there wouldn't be a final bounty to claim, or one last loose end to tie that ended up throwing Taryn back into the cycle of self-doubt and fear.

She could still end up waiting tables at a diner, or sucking big time at a nine-to-five insurance job, but it didn't matter anymore. Lucy would love her, anyway, and Taryn finally realized with some elation that she could even accept herself. She didn't need to give her daughter the big house she'd grown up in, or the fancy schooling. Lucy just wanted Taryn to be her mother. And that was enough for Taryn, too. "I have a little money saved until I find something, and—"

"No, Mom, I was going to say what about that man?"

Taryn's heart constricted and she squeezed Lucy's palm. "He can't hurt you anymore."

"Ouch!" She yanked back her hand, shaking out her fingers. "Not *that* man. The other one. The one who helped you."

Taryn blinked. "Nick?"

"I don't know his name." She yawned.

Taryn thought about distracting Lucy with the M&M's she'd apparently forgotten about. Discussing Nick definitely was not part of the plan. She'd spent a good part of the morning forcing him out of her thoughts. He was probably halfway to Timbuktu by now. Or should be. Taryn didn't have moving that far away in mind.

But she might have, had he asked her.

"Mom? What's wrong?"

Shaken by the sudden direction of her thoughts, she forced a smile for Lucy. "He was just a client, honey, but his case is over. Do you think you can go back to sleep? It's still awfully early."

Lucy nodded and yawned again. "When are we going back to Gramms's house?"

"I'm not sure yet. Let's let her get some sleep for now, okay?"

"Okay," Lucy agreed, her eyes already starting to drift closed.

Olivia probably wasn't getting a minute of sleep at all, Taryn thought as she slowly rose from the couch. But she'd already explained to her mother-in-law that she wasn't quite ready to make herself accessible to the police yet. A couple of files from her computer needed to be erased, and then she had to review the information she'd dug up in the past three days.

Most important, she had to cover her tracks from last night. It wasn't so much herself she was worried about, because she knew most of the detectives downtown. Any questions they had for her were bound to be routine. But she was worried about Nick. And whether anything she'd uncovered would point to evidence of his involvement. Or Dylan Sands's resurrection.

She took one last reassuring look at Lucy before grabbing some change out of her wallet. It was doubtful this morning's *Chronicle* had much to report on what happened last night yet, but she'd take any information she could get. Besides, doing anything to take her mind off Nick was a plus.

Because no matter how many times she reminded herself that for him to disappear again was the only possible happy and safe ending, it still hurt and she already mourned his loss.

To her horror, her eyes started to well as she unlocked the dead bolt. Good thing the newsstand was only a few yards from her office. She blinked several times and dashed away a stray drop of moisture, then opened the door.

She stumbled back in surprise. "Nick?"

He stood on the sidewalk only a foot from the door, looking a little startled himself. His hair was damp and combed back, and he had on a different shirt than he'd worn last night. Hanging from his right hand was a small duffel bag.

His gaze darted past her. "Are you alone?"

"Lucy's here, but she's asleep." She was amazed at how steady her voice sounded considering how hard her heart pounded. "Come in."

"I don't want to wake her."

"You won't. She's on the couch in the back."

He hesitated. "Have the police been here yet?"

She shook her head. "I checked my answering service. They haven't even tried to contact me. Not that I expect them to this soon." She glanced down the dawn-tinted street. The only sign of life was a pair of stockinged feet sticking out of a cardboard box several doors down. "Although I wouldn't suggest you stand out here."

"Right." He seemed preoccupied. Maybe even agitated.

"Where have you been?" she asked, stepping

aside. It was still hard to believe he was actually here, and she had to quash the urge to reach out and touch him as he passed her.

"At my hotel."

"Wasn't that risky?"

"I figured it would look worse if I hadn't picked up my things and checked out. The hotel would end up calling the cops."

"Good point." There was an awkwardness between them that unnerved her. Rubbing her arms, she glanced at the duffel bag. Too small for his clothes. She wasn't sure what that meant. Except that he obviously wasn't planning to stay. Which of course she already knew. She cleared her throat. "I talked to Moose a couple of hours ago."

"Good. Everything okay with him?"

She nodded, shrugged. "He was giving the police a statement when I didn't get an answer at the bar last night. The place is a little torn up but everything else is fine. He doesn't expect the cops will do much. And now that Maynard and Archie are dead..." She shrugged again.

"I'll pay for the damages."

"He'd appreciate that." She smiled a little. "I appreciate it, too."

"It's the least I could do," he said offhandedly. No return smile. Did he feel the awkwardness, too?

Or maybe this encounter was just a loose end for him. And he truly felt nothing.

The thought hit her with staggering sadness, and she struggled against the destructive desire to hang on to him. Physically. Emotionally. "Have you seen today's paper yet?"

"The police have nothing to say." He shrugged.

"No surprise. They have to be chasing their tails, trying to figure out Harrison and Maynard's relationship to Archie. They won't find anything. The agency is thorough, if nothing else."

"What's the media speculating? Burglary gone bad?"

"There really isn't much to the story as far as they're concerned. Maynard hasn't been tied to Harrison or Cain's Imports yet. It probably wouldn't have even made it to the front section of the paper if it wasn't for the fact it happened in a high-rent building."

"One good thing about Houston, huh?" She smiled wryly. "What's one more murder?"

He'd kept his voice low so as not to disturb Lucy, but, glancing over at her snuggled under the peach-colored afghan in the corner, he lowered it still. "Another good reason to get the hell out of here, Taryn."

"What do you mean?" Her pulse skidded, and hope clawed at the needy itch she'd developed since getting to the office. That's why she'd come here, she realized. So he could find her.

His gaze roamed her face, something indefinable darkening his eyes. Something that almost looked like longing as it held her gaze captive for several helpless, wonderful moments, then lowered to linger on her mouth.

God, that's what she wanted it to be. Lust, longing, love. She wanted all of that from Nick Travis.

She stepped closer, feeling his body heat cocoon her and letting the comfort and familiarity of his musky scent strip away the horror of the past twelve hours. If he didn't kiss her soon, she would...

He lifted a hand to cup her shoulder. "Are you

listening, Taryn?'' The desperation in his voice sobered her. Made her curious. The fear in his eyes made her apprehensive. ''This is no place to raise a child. And this is no business for you to be in. Especially not as a single mother.''

''Tell me something I don't know.'' She shrugged, in a show of nonchalance as her mind raced ahead to the possibility of what he might be suggesting.

He dropped the duffel bag and grabbed her other shoulder, his fingers digging into her skin. She automatically jerked at the roughness, but he held her firm, while lowering his head to meet her eyes. She couldn't look away if her life depended on it.

''Promise me, Taryn, promise me you'll—'' He stopped, his expression almost pained, his gaze boring deeply into her. ''Dammit, Taryn,'' he murmured, and pressed his mouth to hers.

She clung to him, kissing him back, hardly daring to believe he was here. Holding her. Allowing her to hope again.

The kiss didn't last long, not nearly long enough for her. When he pulled back, his lips curved in a slow, sensual smile that threatened every bone in her body. He brushed the pad of his thumb across her cheek, then straightened, glancing suddenly toward the couch, as though he'd just remembered they had company. He immediately lowered his hand.

Lucy hadn't stirred an inch. Taryn knew she wouldn't. The kid could sleep through a hurricane. But Nick didn't know that and she appreciated his restraint.

He stepped farther away until they weren't touching at all, and she thought about hauling him back to her. But his entire expression had changed, and he seemed detached, aloof again, and achingly inaccessible.

''I have something for you.'' He picked the duffel bag up off the floor and tried to give it to her. When she didn't take it, he pushed the bag into her hands.

It was fairly heavy, and she instinctively knew what was inside. The knowledge seemed to make the burden even heavier, like a weight, dragging her down to depths so deep she could scarcely breathe. ''What is this?'' she asked.

''Take it, Taryn.''

Resentment welled, making her eyes burn. ''What is this?'' she repeated.

''Give whatever you feel is fair to Moose. The rest is for you.''

Fisting the bag, she held it up between them. She wanted him to spell it out. Admit he was buying her off. ''I asked what this is.''

''A new life.''

''Ah, guilt money.''

''Call it what you want.'' His steely facade faltered, and the wound she'd inflicted fleetingly glinted in his eyes. ''Just promise me you'll get the hell out of here.''

''I don't owe you.'' She dropped the bag at his feet. ''Why should I promise you a damn thing?''

''Because I didn't,'' he said, and she frowned, not understanding. ''I didn't promise you anything because I care about you, Taryn. I never lied to you. Not about us. I knew a happy-ever-after wasn't possible. But I can help you and Lucy start fresh. Let me.''

Damn him. She pressed her lips together and turned away, afraid he'd see the despair in her eyes. Damn him. He was right. She knew there would be no positive outcome. She was the one who'd changed the rules. Because she'd been foolish enough to fall in love with him.

"What about you?" she asked softly, turning back to him.

He half smiled. "Hey, I'll be fine. I'm a chameleon, remember?"

She tried to smile back. It was hard. So damn hard.

"Well," he said, ramming a hand through his hair. It had mostly dried by now, into soft waves she wanted so much to touch. "It's getting light out and I, uh…" He shrugged, then frowned. "What were you doing here, anyway?"

Any illusions she'd had that he'd come to find her shattered. He'd obviously planned to drop off the money and run. "I had to use my computer. Anyway, on the off chance that the police were looking for me already, I knew they wouldn't check here this early."

He studied her for a moment, and then glanced at her computer, the shredded paper that had detailed his case filling her wastebasket. "Thanks."

"For what?"

"Giving me a head start."

She shrugged. "No problem. You paid me well enough."

"Don't, Taryn." His expression turned fierce as he reached for her hand and pulled her close. "I wish I could stay. I wish I could take you with me." He grunted. "And to be honest, in a way, I wish I'd never met you."

Even though she understood, his words hurt. "Now, *you* don't," she said, struggling to keep her voice from shaking. "In a perverse way this experience has been good for me. I'd decided earlier to get out of the business. To leave Houston. For good. No matter what.''

His smile was achingly genuine. "You just made me a very happy man."

"That's not how I'd planned to do it," she admitted with a wry curve of her mouth.

"I know," he said, nodding slowly. "If there was any way—"

She put a finger to his lips to shush him. "I know," she said, echoing his words, finally believing them herself.

"You're going to be fine, Taryn Scott."

"I know that, too." She was proud of the woman she'd become, the mother she was to Lucy, even if her parents weren't.

He studied her eyes, her mouth, tracing her cheek with his thumb, as if trying to memorize everything about her. "I think maybe we both figured out we're human after all, huh? That we don't have to prove anything to anyone but ourselves?" His self-effacing smile wiped the sting from those insightful words, and her defensiveness retreated.

"I'd say we both turned out okay," she agreed, smiling back.

"Not me." His expression was serious. "I say you turned out better than okay." He lowered his mouth to hers.

Outside, a horn blared. Taryn jumped.

Nick cursed. "That's my cab. I had him wait around the corner."

They both glanced at Lucy, who didn't budge.

"I suppose you're headed for the airport," Taryn said, turning back to him, panic rising in her throat when he stared back without answering. "I could give you a ride."

He shook his head with regret. "Better that you don't."

She should have taken comfort in the fact that he looked possibly as miserable as she was, but she didn't. She didn't want him to go. She wanted him to...she wanted *him.*

Without warning, he hauled her against his chest and kissed her hard on the mouth. Just as quickly he put her away from him, desperation, regret, both shadowing his face. "I, um—" He cleared his throat. "You take good care."

"You, too," she whispered, but the second blare of the horn drowned out her words as she watched him head for the door.

When he got there, hesitating with his hand on the knob, he turned back to her. "Look, there's a chance things could work out with the agency. Harrison could have kept some kind of record clearing me of any affiliation with Maynard and Archie's vigilante activities or..." He visibly swallowed and opened the door. "I'll find you."

She watched him disappear, wishing to heaven she could believe him. This time, she didn't.

NICK STOOD ON the sidewalk outside Taryn's office and took several deep breaths. He waved acknowledgment at the cab driver so the guy wouldn't lean on the horn again and send Taryn running out. He didn't think he could handle looking at her for another second.

It hurt too much. Like a dull knife, slowly carving out pieces of his heart.

How could he have so stupidly fallen for her in just four days? It seemed impossible. Except this was Taryn. Tough. Smart. Brave. Loyal. The perfect woman for him. Not that he deserved her. Or that there was any way for them to be together. The agency would take care of that if they found out he was still alive.

Not that life would be worth a damn without Taryn. But he owed her and Lucy a fresh start. They couldn't have that with him in their lives. He'd be an albatross around Taryn's neck. She'd be afraid for him, and right back to looking over her shoulder again.

Judging from the look on her face earlier he figured she'd be willing to risk it as long as Lucy wasn't endangered. But he loved Taryn too much. She deserved unconditional happiness.

He exhaled a long, defeated breath and climbed into the cab. After he gave the driver instructions to take him to the airport, Nick quickly turned his attention out the window. And did something he hadn't done since he was six.

He broke down and cried.

Chapter Seventeen

Three months later

"I'm too old to have a baby-sitter." Lucy flung herself across Taryn's bed and watched her mother apply pink lipstick. "I'm practically eleven."

"Gee, I'll have to buy you a cane for your birthday." Taryn squinted at her reflection in the mirror. Probably too much blush. She picked up a tissue and started blotting.

"Stop it, Mom. You're going to be the prettiest one at the whole PTA meeting."

Taryn's stomach rolled at the mention of attending her first school function. She dropped the tissue in the wastebasket, and smoothing down her tan skirt, she turned to face Lucy. "Do I look okay?"

Lucy sighed. "You look beautiful."

Yeah, but did she look like the other mothers? Taryn turned to frown at her reflection again. Her eyes looked a little tired. Trying to get into the swing of a nine-to-five routine was proving more of a challenge than she'd anticipated. Maybe a little eyeshadow would help.

"You're only going to be gone for two hours, and

Gramms will probably get home from her bridge game before you, anyway. I don't understand why I have to have a baby-sitter.''

"What's the big deal, Luc? You have a boyfriend coming over that I don't know about?''

"Mo-o-om.'' She drawled the word into three syllables and rolled her eyes. "Very funny.''

Taryn smiled, then remembered she'd forgotten to put on earrings and started ransacking her middle dresser drawer in search of the small gold hoops.

Lucy flipped over onto her stomach. "When's dinner? I'm hungry.''

"As soon as the pizza gets here, kiddo. You can have some grapes if you honestly can't wait,'' she said, and Lucy made a face. "No candy bars. Got it?''

"Got it,'' she mumbled, sliding off the bed and shuffling to the door. "I hope you didn't forget to ask for pineapple on the pizza this time,'' she added on her way out, the reminder making Taryn shudder.

Another challenge she hadn't expected. Getting meals on the table at a reasonable hour, making sure Lucy made it to soccer practice and piano lessons on time. Sometimes they had take-out Chinese or fastfood Mexican, probably more often than they should, but Lucy seemed genuinely happy these past three months, and Taryn couldn't ask for anything more.

Well, maybe one thing, she thought wistfully, but she genuinely tried hard not to dwell on Nick.

Especially at night, when she rolled from one side of her lonely queen-size bed to the other, convincing herself that his mysterious scent graced her pillows. And when the old nightmares came, the ones that had plagued her for half her married life, they were different because Nick was always there in the end, pulling her out of the abyss, telling her she would be okay.

They didn't come as frequently anymore, either, and she knew the day would soon arrive when they would stop altogether. She almost regretted that. Nick always seemed so real and present in her life, and she could start the morning pretending.

Except she needed to forget him.

Sometimes the waking hours weren't much easier. Just living in the beautiful four-bedroom English Tudor-style home Nick's money had bought them was reminder enough. If she'd had any idea how much cash had been in the duffel bag, she would never have accepted it. But it was a moot point. It wasn't as though she could return it. She was never going to see Nick again.

"Somebody's here," Lucy yelled from the kitchen. "I don't know if it's the baby-sitter or the pizza guy."

"Don't open the door," Taryn called out. "I'm coming." Hopping on one foot, she slipped a brown leather pump on the other. Damn heels. This, she was never going to get used to, she thought as she hobbled toward the living room.

She pushed the drapes aside and peered outside. A white compact car was parked on the street and a tall man wearing a red baseball hat carried a pizza box up their sidewalk.

Taryn let the drapes fall back into place, relief filling her. The paranoia had waned over the past few months, especially while living in such a quiet Tulsa suburb more than five hundred miles from Houston, but old habits died hard. And she figured it would take a while longer before she could really relax. Not that Lucy would ever be allowed to open the door on her own. Or date until she was thirty.

The doorbell rang as she grabbed her wallet, and she hurried to open the door.

"Pizza delivery for Taryn Scott," the man said in a raspy baritone, the box he held up obscuring his face.

Funny, she hadn't given her first name. And that voice…it sounded sort of familiar. Panic crowded her chest and she stumbled back, ready to slam the door.

He lowered the box.

She gasped. "Nick!"

He smiled, his gaze warm and slightly uncertain. "Who the heck orders pepperoni-and-pineapple pizza?"

"Nick," she whispered this time, slowly shaking her head, half convinced this was a hallucination.

"Yup, I haven't changed it."

She laughed a little when his words sunk in, still shaken from the shock of finding him on her doorstep. "I can't believe you're here."

"I can't believe you ordered pepperoni-and-pineapple pizza."

"That's Lucy." She blinked and turned to see where her daughter was. The end of a long blond ponytail and half a curious face peeked out from the dining room doorway. And then she disappeared.

Taryn knew better than to try to get her to come out right away. Lucy was still shy around men.

"Your pizza is getting cold."

Her gaze flew back to Nick. "Oh, yeah." She stared at him without moving aside, and she realized her mouth was open. Promptly pressing her lips together, she stepped back. "Come in."

He hesitated, his expression serious, his eyes probing. ''The pizza is yours, even if the only tip you have for me is 'get lost.' ''

She could grab him and kiss him. That would be answer enough. But if she touched him, then maybe the spell would be broken and she'd find this was only a dream. Which it had to be. There were too many reasons why he shouldn't be here. Couldn't be here.

''That depends,'' she said finally, ''if you're only planning on staying for five minutes.''

He studied her for a moment, uncertainty again flickering briefly in his eyes. ''Actually, I seem to have a spare forty or fifty years on my hands.''

She blinked, confused, hope and suspicion forming a knot in her chest. His eyes. They weren't dark brown anymore. They were hazel. Like Dylan Sands's. This meant something, but she was too frazzled to think clearly. She only knew he wouldn't be here if he were a danger to them. ''You'd better get in here. Now.''

''Yes, ma'am.'' He lifted the baseball hat off his head once he got inside.

He looked so good. A little tired, maybe even a little thinner, but his hair fell into the same soft waves she remembered in detail and his smile could thaw a glacier. And his shoulders, so broad and… She couldn't go there.

''Just a minute.'' She started toward the kitchen, remembered the pizza, went back and got it from him. ''Go have a seat in the living room. I'll be right back.''

Hiding a smile, she ignored his look of astonishment at what she probably interpreted as dismissal, and went in search of Lucy. What she planned to do to Nick she didn't want her daughter witnessing.

She found her in the kitchen, rummaging through the walk-in pantry, searching for Taryn's candy stash no doubt. "Hey, Luc, the pizza is here," she said, sliding the box onto the kitchen table, then getting a plate out of the cupboard. "You want lemonade with it?"

Lucy popped her head out, her gaze immediately straying toward the door to the dining room. "Where's that man?"

"His name is Nick. Do you remember him?" Taryn asked casually as she got out napkins, a fork and a glass, her heart pounding like crazy.

"I think so. Is he staying for pizza?"

Taryn hoped he was staying for a lot more than that. "I'm not sure. Would you mind if he did?"

Lucy shrugged. "I guess not." She pulled out a kitchen chair and sank into it, eyeing the slice of pizza Taryn slid onto her plate. "As long as I don't have to wait to eat."

"Nope. Dig in." Taryn poured the lemonade. "I'll be right back, okay?"

Lucy nodded. "Are you still going to the PTA meeting?"

"As soon as the baby-sitter gets here."

Lucy sighed and rolled her eyes.

Taryn grinned, then bent down to kiss her cheek. "There's fudge ripple ice cream for dessert."

"Cool." Lucy grinned back around a too-big bite of pizza.

"Don't make yourself sick," Taryn warned with as stern a look as she could muster, considering she was about to kiss Nick senseless.

She headed back for the living room, knowing Lucy would keep herself busy for at least the next ten minutes. When she got there, she found Nick looking at the framed photographs of Lucy at different ages sitting on top of the mantel.

He turned when he heard her approach and opened his mouth to say something. Before he could utter a word, she grabbed him by his shirt and pulled him toward her. A brief grunt of surprise was all he managed before she kissed him so hard he stumbled backward.

When she let him go, he had such a look of utter surprise on his face that she laughed out loud. His gaze narrowed. "Have you been drinking?"

"Heck, no. I have a PTA meeting to go to."

He frowned, but she could tell he was fighting a smile as he eyed her conservative white blouse, the straight tan skirt. "PTA meeting, huh?"

"What's the matter?" She did a slow turn. "You don't like the new me?"

By the time she faced him again, a lazy sensual curve of his mouth sent her pulse racing. "You look so good I could eat you."

That startled another laugh out of her.

This time he grabbed her and pulled her so close her breasts flattened against his chest and she had to tilt her head back to look at him. "I already know you taste better than pepperoni-and-pineapple pizza." His voice was low and gravelly, and she felt moisture immediately pool where it had no business pooling.

Not minutes before she had to go to a PTA meeting, anyway.

"You have a lot to tell me," she whispered, staring into his hazel eyes. The unfamiliar shade should have unnerved her, except they had darkened so much he looked just like the Nick she remembered. The one she'd so often dreamed about.

He nodded and brushed some hair away from her lashes. "Most of it good."

A noise came from the kitchen and they broke apart. The way Nick hurriedly put some distance between them was endearing. She smiled and sat on the couch. He took a chair across the room.

"How's Lucy been doing?" he asked, traces of guilt and shame clouding his features.

"Great. She had some therapy for the first couple of months. I wanted to keep her in longer, but the therapist said Lucy is more well-adjusted than he is." She could hardly believe she was sitting here, talking to Nick in her own living room as if she'd just seen him last week.

"That's because she has such a terrific mother."

Taryn made a face. "Poor kid just wanted a mother, period. But we're okay now. We're doing the usual fighting over homework, and next week is our first bake sale for a soccer fund-raiser." She slid a glance toward the kitchen and sighed. "I may have to enlist Olivia for that one...she lives with us now. Although I don't know. I never saw a woman with such an active social life." Taryn rolled her eyes, belying the fact that she was thrilled for Olivia, who had done so much for Lucy. "I think she may even have a man friend."

"Me, too." Lucy's voice came from behind, startling Taryn. "I think his name is Norman."

Taryn's mouth dropped open. "Really? And how do you know that, young lady?"

Lucy only smiled, her shy gaze darting to Nick.

The fact that she voluntarily showed up while he was still here was a little mind-boggling.

"Hi, Lucy." Nick smiled. "How was the pizza?"

She turned a little pink, but kept the smile. "Awesome. You guys want any ice cream?"

Surprised at her daughter's lack of bashfulness, Taryn started to look at Nick. And then she noticed the time and nearly swore instead. Except she'd given that habit up two months ago. "Where the heck is that baby-sitter? I'm going to be late."

She got up and paced to the window.

Nick cleared his throat. "*I* could keep an eye on Lucy." He cleared it again, and shrugged. "If she doesn't mind."

Taryn's wary gaze went from Nick to her daughter.

"I guess that was a bad idea." He got to his feet, looking uncomfortable.

Taryn pressed her lips together. Obviously he'd misinterpreted her reticence. Of course she trusted him with her daughter for a couple of hours. She'd already trusted him with Lucy's life.

"I don't know." Taryn raised her brows at Lucy. "What do you think?"

Lucy looked timid again, and Taryn hoped she didn't feel put on the spot. But she simply lifted her slim shoulders in a put-out shrug. "I don't care. I just wanted to know if you guys wanted ice cream."

Taryn laughed with both relief and giddiness. "Nick?" He looked confused. "Ice cream? Lucy's buying."

"Does that mean I'm hired?" His eyes met hers. His was full of questions. Uncertainty.

"Yup. You're the official baby-sitter."

"I'd love some ice cream, Lucy," he said, and as

soon as she scurried back to the kitchen, he found Taryn's gaze again. "We haven't negotiated compensation."

She nodded. "I was thinking room and board."

"For how long?" His eyes lit with a smile that made her knees weak.

She swallowed. They had a lot to discuss. Gaps to fill. But she trusted him. He wouldn't be here unless it was safe for him to be. "As long as you want."

His smile started slow but widened to brilliance. "It's all over, Taryn. No more Alpha Agency. Harrison left behind a journal, and between what he'd documented and my testimony, the agency has been dissolved. I promise you'll never have to look over your shoulder because of me."

"What happened to Cross and Syd?"

"Cross has a desk job in D.C. Syd bought some ocean front property in Mexico and is taking an extended vacation with his family. Remember that doll we found that I hoped was for his niece? Turns out his niece is really his daughter. He'd managed to keep that a secret."

She had so many questions. "What about the others in New York who worked for Archie?"

"One's dead. The other will be making license plates for the rest of his life."

She didn't want to know how the man had met his end. "What if the government decides you're still a risk?"

"Then I guess they won't mind having the entire story plastered across the front page of the *New York Times*." One side of his mouth lifted. "I truly don't think they're interested in me anymore, but I have taken certain safeguards of which they're well aware."

Taryn started to smile. "So now you just deliver pizzas."

He chuckled. "It cost me fifty bucks to intercept that sucker."

She slowly left her seat. "One more thing before I leave." He lifted a brow. "I'm gonna have to frisk you."

His eyes darkened, and his voice lowered. "Yeah? Sure you don't need me to strip?"

"I put your ice cream in a cone, if that's okay." Lucy's voice coming from the dining room made them both straighten.

Taryn grinned. "Guess you're going to have to hold that thought."

* * * * *

Look for Debbi Rawlins's next book,
LOVING A LONESOME COWBOY
coming from Harlequin American Romance
January 2001!

What can be stolen, forgotten, hidden, replaced, imitated—but never lost?

HARLEQUIN®

I N T R I G U E®

brings you the strong, sexy men
and passionate women who are
about to uncover...

SECRET IDENTITY

LITTLE BOY LOST
by Adrianne Lee
August 2000

SAFE BY HIS SIDE
by Debra Webb
September 2000

HER MYSTERIOUS STRANGER
by Debbi Rawlins
October 2000

ALIAS MOMMY
by Linda O. Johnston
November 2000

Available at your favorite retail outlet.

HARLEQUIN®
Makes any time special ™